Angels on Overtime

A divine romantic comedy

Ann Crawford

Published by Lightscapes Publishing
Distributed by Bublish, Inc.
Cover by AM Designs Studios

ISBN: 978-1-948543-20-0 (paperback)
ISBN: 978-1-948543-25-5 (eBook)

For

Marion

A QUESTION

There's a saying that every single blade of grass has an angel bending over it, gently whispering, "Grow! Grow! Grow!"

If every single blade of grass has that much loving attention, can you imagine what every single human being has?

You're about to find out.

CHAPTER 1

Once upon a time in a galaxy far, far away—oh, sorry, that's another story. But it could be this one, too. Could be the beginning of a lot of stories. All stories, really. But actually the galaxy isn't far, far away, because nothing is far, far away, really...everything is just a thought away. Everything.

So in this galaxy that isn't very far away after all is a very large room. Very large. Emphasis on very. And large. Oh, you wouldn't believe the love and dedication that fills this room! This room spreads on for miles and miles and miles in every direction. You can't even see its walls. But more about the room itself in a little bit. Right now we're standing in front of an office. The sign on the office door reads MANAGER, ANGELIC AF-FAIRS—which makes no sense at all, really, because everything, everywhere would fall under the category of affairs of angels. And we'd all be managers managing them. But anyway....

Henry, a plump, balding angel sits behind his large, angelifical desk. Now you might wonder why this angel would choose to be plump and balding and sitting behind a large, angelifical desk when he can choose to be anything, anywhere. Well, what do you think of when you see a plump, balding man? Wasn't your favorite uncle like that? How about your favorite, old art teacher in that frumpy, navy-blue cardigan with the frayed elbows? And didn't you just want to throw your arms around him in a big, sloppy bear hug? Well, that's why Henry chooses to be plump and balding, and why anyone would choose to be plump and balding—because it's all a choice. All of it, every last bit—it's a choice. Maybe the choice isn't made consciously, top-of-mind, but it's made. Not sure how many big, sloppy bear hugs Henry, your uncle, or that old art teacher actually got, but I'm sure lots of folks thought about it.

Now as for sitting behind his desk, that's another choice, because, as you now well know, anyone can be anything, anywhere. But Henry chooses to sit behind his large, angelificial desk to be of high service. And since he is a very organized angel and loves being an Angelic Resources Manager (you know, like the best Human Resources Manager in the best organization you ever worked for?), that's what he chooses. And he chooses the angelificialness of his angelificial desk to weed out the ones who don't really mean it. The chaff from the wheat. The angels from the, well, angels. Okay, the less-than-dedicated angels from the highly dedicated angels.

Henry looks to be about sixty-five—in Earth Time. Sitting in front of him is Brooke. Now Brooke is what you might picture an angel to look like...if an angel could be of Northern European descent, anyway: long, blond hair and big, blue eyes that soak in the worlds around her. She appears to be about twenty-five in Earth Time. But really, she's as old as the universe. And so are you, by the way. Put in that perspective, you've been holding up very well. It's truly amazing how wonderful everyone looks, considering.

Do angels have wings? Well, they do if they want to. Brooke and Henry don't have them, nor do any of the angels in our story here, but many an angel or two have donned a pair of wings for that special occasion or two or eighteen million when they wanted to look especially angelic.

"Why would you want to do this?" Henry demands of Brooke. "It's the hardest job in the universe!"

"It's all you hear about," Brooke answers, "all over every single galaxy: Earth, Earth, Earth. I figure if I can't get in as a human, I could try it this way."

"These humans can be as thick as wood. And just as pliable." Henry looks at her over the top of his bifocals. Angels sometimes wear bifocals when they want to have that professorial look, too, just like humans. "Why don't you go to Arcturus and just be content with peace, love, and instant manifestation?"

"This is what I want. More than anything in the entire universe."

Henry sighs. "Alright then. Follow me. It's not like we couldn't use a willing volunteer down there." But he smiles to himself, as if at some joke.

Henry leads Brooke out the door and through a tiny part of that seemingly infinite room. In thousands upon millions upon billions of cubicles, thousands upon millions upon billions of angels sit at their computer desks in groups of three, sometimes four, and sometimes two groups of three or four sitting side by side with numerous monitors in one bigger cubicle. The room has a distinct thrum as it hums with the voices of these thousands upon millions upon billions of angels. If you heard this thrum, you'd realize that, well, you do hear this thrum. All the time. The Earth has this thrum, the galaxies have this thrum, the universe has this thrum, and you have this thrum. The thrum is everywhere, resonating in one universal harmonic.

At first glance, a first-timer—which would be you—might think that the room's vibrant radiance comes from the monitors and other external light sources. But a second glance would inform you that the monitors are actually somewhat dim and there are no other light sources. Oh, what love and devotion in billions of angels can do. Just imagine what love and devotion in seven billion—well, we're getting ahead of ourselves here.

Henry and Brooke pass two angels conferring over their computer monitors while the third in their triumvirate whispers softly into a microphone.

"No, no," one angel says to the other. "You can't have them meet yet. They're supposed to have a child that's going to be the Senator of Tennessee in 2067, and they can't conceive her until after the accident, which can't happen for another two years."

Brooke looks at Henry in surprise. If she were one of your teenagers, I believe she would be saying, "WTF?"

Before Henry can say anything, the second angel answers the first: "Okay, let's send this schlub along. That'll keep her occupied for a little while."

The first angel appears shocked. "Schlub?"

"Okay, okay," the second angel replies, somewhat abashed, "a drop of divinity cleverly disguised as a schlub."

Brooke again turns to Henry. "They do this while their assignment sleeps?"

"Right. Their assignment is obviously a late sleeper. Could be a hooker." And then, to the surprise on her face, "Not to worry, it's all good. It's all a divine path."

He leads Brooke past a closed office door. RAIN-DANCERS, the elaborate sign announces.

"Raindancers?"

"Oh," Henry shakes his head, "you'd be amazed at how many humans want to rain on their own parade, keep worrying about nonsense, look at the bad side of anything. Raindancers only perform when asked, but they are in hot demand. You want to be extra busy, sign up for Raindancing." And to her still-surprised expression, he adds, "It's all good."

Henry and Brooke continue walking and arrive at a bank of elevators. While Henry presses the down button, Brooke notices a very serious angel nearby, closely watching graphs and trends appear on his computer screen. His piercing blue eyes, which peer out from under hooded eyelids, look like they belong in a bird of prey, not in an angel.

"What's his gig?"

Henry puts his fingers to his lips, imploring that she keep her voice down. "Karmic enforcer," he whispers. "A job nobody wants. They have to recruit from the dark side."

"Dark side? There's no such thing!"

"Tell *him* that. Anyone in creation can believe anything he or she wants to and create that reality."

"But—"

"And he's found a lot of people on Earth willing to participate in that reality."

"Yuck!"

Henry leans close to Brooke's ear. "Don't tell him this, or the humans who want to participate, but karma can be changed the instant the intent to change it is there." Henry stops for a moment to consider what he just said. "Actually, no, my mistake—your job *is* to tell humans that. It'll save them a *lot* of time. If they can hear you, that is."

Ping! The elevator arrives and they hop aboard. Out of two hundred and fifty buttons with different codes, letters, and numbers, Henry locates E.

"E for Earth," he tells her. "But it's not too late to choose A for Arcturus or S for Sirius."

"I'm good with E," Brooke responds.

"Just double-checking." Henry presses the E button and turns to Brooke. "Love and remember. Love and wake up. That's *all* these humans have to do. And you'd be amazed how many mountains they put in their own way."

The elevator departs from the enormous angelic hall—okay, it's really part elevator, part rocket ship—and shuttles across the galaxies. Brooke gasps as the beautiful blue orb of Earth appears through the window. "Oh!"

"Beautiful, isn't it? One of the finest creations in the universe. And they insist on decimating it, even though they have alternatives."

The shape of North America appears in the window, and in just a matter of seconds, California appears to be rushing up to meet them.

"But they'll get it," Henry assures her. "That's their job—to get it—and they have eternity."

"They do?"

"If not here, somewhere. But it would be a shame to waste this incredible creation. Do what you can about that, okay?"

"Absolutely." Brooke gasps again as the Southern California coast is now right beneath them.

"Are you ready?"

"Yes."

"What?"

"Yeah!"

"What?"

"Yeah!"

"What?"

"YES!"

"You sure?"

"I'm sure."

"You sure you're sure?"

"I'm SURE I'm sure!"

THUD! The elevator lands on E. The elevator door opens and Brooke is too surprised even to gasp. They have landed in a small patch of grass by the 405 Freeway, somewhat near the Los Angeles airport. The trees, leaves, and grass shimmer and radiate with their own internal light. From Brooke and Henry's vantage point, the veil has been lifted, and bending over every single blade of grass is an angel whispering, "Grow! Grow! Grow! Thank you for being here. You are so loved. You are such a blessing. You are a miracle."

As Brooke looks up and down the freeway, she sees more and more areas of grass, and she marvels at the amazingly stunning sight of more and more angels becoming visible to her.

The freeway is completely clogged. The cars are lit up by the light of the human occupants inside of them. But the exhaust from each car and the smog that hangs over the city seems to move, even dance, in a demonic way.

"What—what are they doing to themselves? Can't they see what they're doing?"

"It's just wild how much denial humans can put themselves in. All of some can see, and part of the others can see, but they suppress it. It'll be part of your job to help all of all of them see." To Brooke's confused expression, Henry adds, "You'll see what I mean, all in good time."

He gently takes her by the arm, and they float over the cars. "We landed a little too far east," he tells her. "We have to cross over the freeway to that neighborhood over there." The houses he points to are barely visible through the thick smog.

Brooke becomes aware of something that sounds like a beehive. And the beehive is growing louder and louder. As they glide over the freeway, she peers through the car windows. Inside each vehicle, accompanying but completely unbeknownst to the humans, are three angels—two are sitting beside their human and the third is in the backseat consulting a laptop computer.

A seriously suntanned man with a seriously bad hairdo shakes his fist out the window of his BMW to the driver that just cut him off.

"Goddamn son of a bitch! Where in the world did you learn to drive—on a farm?"

"Actually," Henry chuckles to Brooke, "the answer to that is yes."

They float over the car next to the boorish Beamer driver to find a woman who appears to be very composed—almost as if she's about to step onto a ballroom dance floor. But inside her head, her thoughts are going a mile a minute.

"Oh, why didn't I tell him what I really wanted to say? Why did I say what I said? What was I thinking? Should I call him and tell him what I really wanted to say? Oh, how could I have done that? What should I do?"

"Ouch!" Brooke winces, although she can't feel pain. But she feels compassion—that's her job. "That must hurt!"

"Oh, yes," Henry sighs, "it does. Quite a bit. Takes most of 'em a long time to learn that—if they ever do, that is."

The beehive, Brooke realizes, is really the cacophony of millions upon millions of thoughts drifting up to her.

Brooke and Henry float over the next car, where the driver is singing to his dashboard. "I'm too sexy for my shirt, too sexy for my shirt!"

They float over the next car, where the driver is doing the exact same thing. "I'm too sexy for my shirt, too sexy for my shirt."

Puzzled, Brooke turns to Henry. "That sounded a little different."

"He was singing in Japanese. But you can understand everything, everywhere."

"Why aren't their angels talking to them, any of them?" Brooke asks.

"How in the world could they hear their angels if their minds are so overly overactive?"

They float over another car and no thoughts float up to them.

"She must've meditated this morning," Henry answers Brooke's quizzical look. "And every morning for the past thirty years."

Brooke notices the woman has four angels sitting in meditation around her. "So why aren't her angels talking? They could get through to her."

"No need," Henry replies. "She's on her right path. They speak to her from time to time just for a touch of guidance and reassurance."

One of the angels opens one eye to look at the graphs on her laptop and then returns to her meditation. One of the other angels breaks from his meditation to address the woman: "Thank you for all that you do. You're such a blessing." As the woman smiles, the angel returns to his meditating.

"See?" Henry says to Brooke. "Actually, every single person on Earth has an angel who says that, over and over, when he or she can get through all the noise of the TV, radio, and the human's own thoughts. But, even then, so few hear it."

They float over another car with two people inside and six angels accompanying them. The radio is blaring loudly. The angels have their hands over their ears.

Brooke notices one lone angel over one lone blade of grass growing through a crack in the concrete by the freeway.

"Grow! Grow! Grow!" whispers the angel. "You're a miracle. Thank you for being here. You're such a blessing to us all."

They float over the freeway wall, and Brooke sees an entirely different world as they glide down an attractive, tree-lined street of lovely, little homes with tidy, freshly mowed yards and well-tended gardens. Henry leads her to one particular house with requisite tidy yard along with innumerable angels talking to each blade of grass, each flower, even each leaf on a shrub.

"When it gets too much," he tells her, "just fade them. You're not even seeing all the dimensions. Even I don't, when I can avoid it. It'd make you crazy if you did. But if you do want to see other dimensions, just choose. The choice is always there."

The angels in the yard fade away as Brooke makes that choice.

The two voyagers float into the house. A pile of shoes greets them and piles of who-knows-what line the foyer. They float down the hallway and into a large family room off the kitchen. Now if you had just walked into the room, you would see a man playing with his young son and a woman potatoing on the couch to an early-morning quasi-news show. And if you could see like an angel, you would see the three humans and nine other beings in the room—a committee of three angels for each human. And that's not counting the angels for the plants around the room, who are working even more intensely because their charges haven't been watered in weeks.

Jack. Ohhhhh, Jack. He's the man playing with the little boy. Yikes—you just want to grab him by those tightly hunched shoulders and shake him loose! The only thing tighter than his clenched fists is his jawline. Jack could be very handsome if he weren't so sad. And even if you weren't particularly sensitive, and even if it was a rare moment when Jack had a smile on his face, you'd still know he's sad. You could feel it, even across the room. If you were to take one look at him, you'd probably want to close your eyes so you could reenvision him as a strong, beautiful, powerful man—what he *could* be, perhaps what his original blueprint depicted about thirty-five years ago.

"But it's kind of like someone came along and deflated the balloon of his being," Brooke says.

"If someone else actually has that power," Henry replies. "Which no one does."

Three angels surround Jack: Christopher, Sapphire, and Blake. Your quintessential computer geek, Christopher wears glasses over his sharp, black eyes (yes, as you probably already surmised, angels wear glasses, too, when they want to proudly present that intellectual look). His ebony skin contrasts against his red and blond Mohawk—even angelic geeks like to sport that alternative look from time to time. Christopher constantly studies his laptop to watch graphs, analyze trends, make mental notes from the running tick of information gathered from all corners of the universe, and calculate statistics. On occasion, he looks up from his computer, but it has to be quite the occasion—which you know will happen because you certainly wouldn't be reading a book about a non-occasion. But basically picture an angelic actuarial services analyzer albeit from the very hip part of town, and Christopher's your guy...well, your angel.

Sapphire whispers into Jack's ear. She's the sweet librarian type—you remember that truly great librarian, the one you wondered about and asked your friends if they thought she had a life? At least a life that didn't involve reference desks and card catalogs? Or for those of you younger ones who have never researched away from the Internet and are wondering what in creation a card catalog could possibly be, picture instead a woman who loves to look on her computer to see what wisdom is found where. At any rate, this librarian from your hometown library just loved researching things and helping you find information. She was born to work in a library, and you thought, wow, it's *really* good we're all interested in such different things, so it all gets taken care of. (And yes, everyone thought she had a very boring life, but oh how wrong they were—you wouldn't *believe* the life she had!) Behind Sapphire's thick glasses and tightly wound bun, she is actually very, very beautiful.

They're all beautiful. Honestly, have you ever seen an ugly angel? Or, if you've never seen an angel, have you ever imagined an ugly one? Impossible. Just like humans. Maybe there are some less-than-attractive humans, but most are pleasant looking. A small percentage fall in the absolutely-breathtakingly-beautiful category and an even smaller percentage fall in the far-less-than-absolutely-breathtakingly-beautiful category. But they're all beautiful—all angels, all humans. You know what we mean.

Sapphire's job is to whisper continuously in Jack's ear, which is exactly what she's doing now. And what does she whisper? A compendium that goes something like this: "Jack, you are so beautiful. You are loved. You are a blessing. Thank you for being here. Thank you for blessing us. Jack, you are such a wonderful being. Jack, you are loved. You are so dear. You are such a blessing. Thank you for all that you do."

Well, you get the idea. Everyone, everywhere on Earth, has an angel whispering to him or her like that. So why isn't life a steady stream of perfection? Because very few can hear these words. But that's starting to change, at least here and there.

Next to Christopher and Sapphire stands Blake. Remember your favorite high-school coach? Well, he probably was very Blake-like. "Atta boy," or "Atta girl," he'd say to you when you did a particularly good maneuver on the playing field. Or, if sports were not your thing, he'd say, "Nice try, kid." And you'd know that while he didn't understand how in the world sports weren't first and foremost in your every thought, he really could tell you tried, and he sure did appreciate that.

Blake pats Jack on the shoulder. "Jack, you're a wonderful father. You're a wonderful businessman. But you know what? There's more for you to do, son." He pats him again—if Jack could've actually felt that pat, he probably would've fallen over.

"Hey!" Christopher exclaims, watching a graph on his computer. "Check it out—his awareness just went off the charts! I think he heard you. It looks like he might finally be getting it—no, no, forget it...just a passing thought."

"Nah, he didn't hear me," Blake says. "His heart is open from playing with his little boy. You've seen this before—happens every day when he's with him. With his baby girl, too. But it doesn't stay."

Meanwhile, Sapphire simply whispers in Jack's ear: "You are so dear. You are such a blessing. Thank you for all that you do."

"Jack, Jack, Jack," Blake practically hollers to him, clapping his hands. He bends over next to him, hand on Jack's shoulders, like a coach trying to pep up a reluctant-but-necessary player sitting on the bench. "It's time to run with the ball, son. Time to know there's even a ball in play. Time to know you're even on the ball field. Time to know there's even a game going on!"

Henry looks at the clock on the mantle. "He'll be off to work soon," he tells Brooke, "but he's getting as much as he can of the most joyous thing in his life before he drops him off at preschool. One of the most joyous things, anyway. The other joy is his daughter. And this is Lacey, his wife," he says, pointing to a form that has very successfully merged with the couch.

Brooke glances over at Lacey, who's still doing the most wonderful job of potatoing. Yes, well, everyone on Earth has his or her special talent, and if a higher talent isn't cultivated and nurtured, the lowest common denominator talent tends to prevail. Lacey might have been prettier in her day, and she could be on this day, if she wanted to be. Nope, doesn't want to be: the bulge is winning this particular battle, dark roots are taking over the blond in her stringy, shoulder-length hair, her hazel eyes have long gone slack.

Surrounding Lacey are her three angels. If this team's computer aficionado was from Earth, you would think she's from Southeast Asia, and she'd be gorgeous if she weren't so bored. She watches Lacey for a moment and then sighs as she starts to play a game of solitaire on her computer. There aren't too many charts to watch when the human is so, well, uninvolved with life.

A chubby, adolescent-looking angel plays paddleball while an even younger-looking angel plays jacks on the floor. Adorable? Off the charts.

"Have they given up on her?" Brooke asks.

"Oh, no," Henry answers. "But they have to wait 'til she turns off the TV. They'll work on her when she gets up to use the bathroom. Can't work on people while their minds are fully occupied with rot."

"Why such young angels for her?"

Henry laughs. "Those two are ageless, timeless, eternal beings, just like all of us. But young-looking ones tend to act more young-at-heart. Sometimes angels like that are the only ones who can reach people like Lacey here. Special assignment."

Brooke looks over at the couple's son.

"And that's Ben, their three-year-old."

Ben's three angels huddle around him, devoted to their tasks for him. (You'll never see an angel working hard, but always with immense devotion and diligence.) One whispers in his ear, one studies her computer, one watches Ben carefully.

"You are so loved," whispers Ben's whisperer into his ear. "You are such a light. You have so much to give." A smile spreads across Ben's face.

Brooke glances into the kitchen. Piles of dishes from meals obviously long past sit in the sink, drops of milk and cereal decorate the placemats on the table, and there are more piles of that who-knows-what everywhere. Brooke notices that piles even surround Lacey on the couch.

Brooke points to Jack. "So he's my assignment?"

"In living color," Henry says.

Brooke watches Jack as he and Ben work on their creation, a dinosaur made of Legos. Giggling, Ben adds pieces of Legos in the shape of what you could guess is an elephant's trunk. Jack chuckles. Wow! His shoulders start to move down to a level far more appropriate for a human shoulder. Lacey laughs—snorts, really—as a television announcer jokes, however; even though he doesn't look up at her, Jack's shoulders zoom right back up to his ears and his jawline goes rigid again.

"He doesn't exactly flow with the go," Brooke sighs.

"Go with the flow," Henry corrects her. But he ponders for a moment. "Actually, I like it better your way."

"Oh, Jack," Brooke whispers to him, this man who clearly could be so very handsome and vibrant, but for some reason lives far, far below where he could be living. His son looks like a happier version of him in miniature: curly brown hair, big brown eyes, irrepressible smile. As Ben adds a giraffe's neck to the dinosaur,

Jack's demeanor softens and relaxes—until Lacey snorts again, that is.

"At bottom, everything is a choice," Henry says. "Everything."

In another office, another sign on the office door reads MANAGER, ANGELIC AFFAIRS. Penelope, a middle-aged (in Earth Time), plump-and-pleasant angel sits behind her angelificial desk while David, another neophyte, sits in front of her.

Now David also looks like what you might picture an angel to look like, if you were to picture an angel who looks like the blending of the nations of Earth. He has caramel-colored skin, large dark-brown eyes, the blackest hair. You can see Africa in his eyes, Europe in his facial features, the subcontinent in his mannerisms, the Americas in his build, Asia in his hair. That's if his ancestors really came from all those places, which they could have, if they were humans. But, really, we all come from the same thing: Life. Actually, David has come to this galaxy via the far side of the Carina Nebula, if you must know. He looks to be about twenty-eight or so in Earth Time.

"Why would you want to do this?" Penelope demands of him. "It's the hardest job in the universe!"

David musters his moxie. "It's all anyone can talk about—here, there, everywhere: Earth. Earth. Earth. The line is way too long—light-years!—to get in as a human, so I figured I'd try it this way."

"These humans can be absolutely impossible. You know that, don't you? Sometimes they just refuse to get it, even after several thousand lifetimes. Why don't you go to Sirius and just be content with peace, love, and instant manifestation?"

"This is what I want to do," David insists. "More than anything in the universe."

"Alright then," Penelope sighs. "Follow me. It's not like we couldn't use a willing volunteer down there." But she smiles to herself, as if at some joke.

Penelope leads David through a tiny part of the infinite room with the thousands upon millions upon billions of cubicles with the thousands upon millions upon billions of angels at their computer terminals—a different part of the room than the one you saw Henry and Brooke walk through. They pass two angels conferring over their computer screens while a third whispers into a microphone. The upper-left monitor exhibits a young man sleeping.

"As you can see," Penelope explains, "a lot of this computing and arranging happens while their assignment sleeps. This guy is a late sleeper! Could be a drug dealer." She turns around to look at David for a second. "It's all simply divine," she says to the look of surprise on his face. "Everything, every last thing, can be a path of awakening."

"Isn't most of this planned out before they incarnate?" David asks.

"Often their main lessons are planned, yes. But as for the details, well, the future is always in constant motion," Penelope says. "Always. Their lives can change at any instant, depending on a change in intention, a new belief, a sudden cracking open and waking up, or anything at all."

They pass another cubicle where two more angels confer quietly; a third angel speaks into a microphone as she watches a monitor, which reveals a sleeping woman. "You are a miracle," she whispers softly. "You are a blessing. You are so very loved."

"Few of them remember hearing that when they wake up," Penelope says, "and even fewer hear it during their waking hours."

Penelope leads David past an office door. EXTRA SUPPLIES OF INERTIA, the sign on the door reads.

"Extra supplies of inertia?"

"You'd be amazed at what these humans call in to slow themselves down. Popular item, that."

They continue walking and pass another set of three angels; two are studying a computer while the third one whispers into a microphone.

The first angel points to a monitor. "Well, she said she was here to help her daughter, no matter what. And," she fast-forwards through some recorded snippets on the monitor, "her daughter is looking for a conscious cowboy."

The second angels sputters. "A conscious cowboy?"

"Well, there must be one somewhere," the first angel responds.

The third angel pauses in his whispering and turns to them. "Oh, you'd be surprised at how many conscious cowboys there are. They just don't advertise it." He returns to his whispering.

"Texas *is* a big state," the first angel remarks, just thinking out loud. "Hmmmmmm...."

Penelope and David pass cubicle after cubicle with similar tableaux and arrive at the elevator. Penelope presses the down button while, nearby, three more angels study their main computer screen as a fourth angel whispers.

"How many angels does each human get?" David asks.

"Everyone has at least three. When they're ready to wake up, that's when they get their fourth, because the workload has just increased dramatically."

"For them or us?"

"Yes."

Ping! The elevator arrives and they climb aboard. Out of two hundred and fifty buttons with different codes, letters, and numbers, Penelope locates E. She pauses before she pushes it. "E for Earth. It's still not too late to choose A for Arcturus or S for Sirius."

"I'm good with E," David says.

Penelope presses E and turns to him. "Love and remember. Love and wake up. That's *all* these humans have to do. And you'd be amazed how many twists and turns they put in their own roads."

"Wow!" David exclaims as the beautiful blue orb of Earth appears in the window of their elevator/rocket ship.

"A jewel, isn't it? One of the masterpieces of the universe. Well, everything is a masterpiece, of course, but this is the masterpiece of masterpieces."

Through the bottom of the elevator, the mountains of Idaho zoom into focus.

"But they'll get it," Penelope says. "That's their job—to get it—and they have eternity."

"They do?"

"If not here, somewhere."

The mountains of Idaho are now right beneath them. Penelope turns to David and brushes some unseen angel lint off his shoulders and fluffs up his aura. "Are you ready?"

"Yes."

"What?"

"Yeah."

"What?"

"Yeah."

"What?"

"YES!"

"You sure?"

"I'm sure."

"You sure you're sure?"

"I'm SURE I'm sure!"

THUD! The elevator lands on E. The door opens and David gasps. From their vantage point, the veil is lifted and they can see a field of grass—and every single blade of grass has an angel bending over it, whispering, "Grow! Grow! Grow! Thank you for being here. You're such a blessing. You are a miracle. Grow! Grow! Grow!"

David looks toward the horizon and sees more and more angels tending to their tender charges, a single blade of grass. The trees have thousands of angels hovering around them, one whispering to each leaf. Beneath the angelic whispering is a deeper hum.

"That's from the trees," Penelope explains. "Powerful beings, those trees."

David spots a lone car traveling down a country road. He and Penelope can see the driver, a very forlorn and extremely overweight—obese, really—woman in her fifties with three angels around her. Two talk to the woman while the third consults her computer. A half-eaten bag of donuts sits in the woman's lap, and she brushes crumbs away from her mouth. A strange, somewhat bluish light shimmers all around her billowing body.

"You are so beautiful," the first angel whispers to her. "You are so very beautiful. You are a gift. You are a blessing. You are a miracle. You are so beautiful."

"You are so beautiful," the second angel whispers. "You are so beautiful. You are so beautiful."

"You are so, so beautiful," the first angel continues. "You are a gift. You are so beautiful. You are a blessing. You are so beautiful."

The computer-watcher angel puts her computer down and starts to whisper, as well. "You are so beautiful. You are a gift."

The car disappears over a hill, but not before David witnesses a tear running down the woman's face as she reaches for another donut.

"All three were whispering."

"Yes. Special case."

"Will she ever hear them?"

"It's up to her. You sure you want to do this?"

For the first time, David hesitates before answering, but then delivers a very firm, "Yes."

"Yours will be a little easier than that one," Penelope assures him.

David sighs with relief. "Oh, good."

"A little little."

"Oh."

Penelope and David float by a nearly deserted gas station and convenience store on the side of the road. A robber points a gun at the store owner, who grabs at the cash in the register. Both have a group of three angels, all speaking to their respective human.

The robber's lead angel tries to appeal to him. "You can do better than this! It's time to give up your habit!"

The robber's second angel speaks to the store owner's angels. "Tell him to say something that will reach him!"

The store owner's first angel speaks to him, referring to the robber. "Tell him he can do better than this! Tell him he can get help for his addiction!"

The terrified store owner throws a fistful of cash to the robber, who shoves the money in his pocket and then bolts. All six angels groan, throwing their hands up in frustration. The robber's angels disappear out the door as the man dashes to his car.

The store owner pauses and then runs to the doorway. "You can get help to get off drugs you know!" he yells after the robber.

After a moment of surprise, his angels high five, fist bump, and hug each other. "Yes!" one shouts.

"But he said it too late," David says to Penelope.

"But it shows that he heard them, that they got through to him, which is over ninety-nine percent of the challenge. And they both have eternity to get it all, so nothing is ever too late."

The two angels float over a few tree-covered hills and dales until they arrive at a cozy mountain home, which has the usual assemblage of angels standing over every blade of grass.

"When that gets overwhelming, just fade it out," Penelope whispers to David. "Choose whatever you want to see."

The angels disappear and the lawn just radiates as David makes his choice. He looks off in the distance to a neighbor's yard, an eyesore of brown grass and bare patches.

"They're there, too," Penelope says.

As he makes a new choice, David notices the angels over that lawn, too, whispering to the dead grass. He fades them out.

"Lifting the different veils can get too much for us angels, too," Penelope warns. "All the fairies flittering about. All the dead people wandering around. Even the bugs have bug angels. Just make the choice of what you want to see."

David turns his attention back to the house. What a darling place! The two levels make it seem like an overgrown cottage. The screened-in porch around it looks almost like arms reaching out and hugging the little home. Red geraniums sit in a terra-cotta pot on each step leading up to the front door. A flower garden surrounds the house, and along the garden pathway there's even a little archway bedecked with morning glories. Queen Anne's lace covers almost the entire lawn. And a white picket fence—of course—surrounds the whole storybook picture.

David and Penelope float into the house, where they find Emily cooking breakfast. David does a double take. How could this precious home belong to someone who is so, so, so......sad? For she is so very, deep down, seemingly irrevocably sad. Just looking at her makes David want to cry—if he could cry, that is.

"Meet Emily and her husband Sam," Penelope says.

Sam slumps at the kitchen table, hiding behind the paper. David looks back at Emily. Oh, but she's a beauty. Or she could be. Her enormous blue eyes seem to be pleading for something from the world. Her long, chestnut-brown hair is braided in one thick plait. Her tight jeans and t-shirt reveal a thin frame. Willowy is the word invented to describe Emily, but willowy with some strong sap running through its limbs. Strong, but unused at present.

Now Sam, on the other hand, might have been a good-looking, strapping man not that long ago, but now he's something else. His sap has gone and gotten itself sticky, stale, and stiff. Sawdust covers him from his baseball cap to his work boots. His blue jeans are, well, not so very blue. The pepper of his slightly longish hair is still in the race, but the salt will be taking the lead soon. He looks like he's seen his share of decades come and go, perhaps one more than Emily has.

David notices the two angel committees surrounding their human assignments. The computer geek for Emily's angel team smiles at him. "Stephanie's the name."

"David."

"I know." Stephanie pushes her thick glasses back up to the bridge of her nose and turns back to the kaleidoscope of charts on her laptop. She's not unfriendly, really; it's just that, like some people, she prefers to stay on task and keep any extraneous frivolities to a minimum. Expeditious would be a good word to describe her. And the thick glasses? A fun prop.

A bubbly, heavyset, middle-aged-looking woman holds her hand out to David. "Angela," she announces. "Jolly good to meet you." She speaks in what you would consider an accent from the British Isles. After shaking her hand, David watches a boyish, almost adolescent-looking angel whisper in Emily's ear. "And that's Jasper," Angela says.

"You are so dear," Jasper whispers. "You are such a blessing. Thank you for all that you do."

"Excellent job on breakfast this morning, Emily," Angela chimes in. "And you were a wonderful friend, too, when Beth's call came in. But there's so much more awaiting you."

Stephanie consults a newly emerging chart. "Emily, you could be a really savvy businesswoman if you wanted. Just look at how amazing you are with numbers, when you want to be."

"There's far more for you to do, my dear," Angela states. "When would you like to begin? How about today? Wouldn't that be a good idea?"

David looks across the room to Sam's angel team. He tries to hide his surprise when he spots an angel who appears to be a fat, lazy slob on the team. Could there be fat, lazy slob angels? Well, sure there could—in appearances.

"They won't be too friendly to you," Penelope whispers. "They know you're here to help advance Emily, which means that pretty soon she'll be too much for Sam to handle, which means they'll have more work on their hands. Just having her in Sam's life deflects a lot of work for them."

"Yo, Sam," Sam's angel team leader says, "we'll talk to you when you put that paper down, bud. Any day now." David can tell that the leader is talking mostly by rote; it's not that angels stop believing in their human projects, but even angels get weary.

"You are so dear," Sam's whisperer whispers, mostly to herself. "You are such a blessing. Thank you for all that you do." She stops as Sam becomes more engrossed in an ad. David notices that it's not even a newspaper—it's a paper of classified ads.

"Can't we talk to them while they're reading?" David asks Penelope. "Or even through the paper itself?"

"Sometimes," Penelope answers. "Depends on the person. Apparently not this one."

Sam's angelic whisperer straps on a pair of roller skates and skates around the kitchen. Oh sure, she could fly around the room if she wanted to, but angels like to do other things, too, at times. Don't laugh— stranger things have happened. You've seen stranger things happen, on more than just a couple of occasions. Okay, laugh.

Emily's kitchen is spotless, even in the midst of her breakfast-making. Shiny, copper-bottomed pots dangle from a rack over the stove, bright hand-woven pot-holders hang on nearby hooks, and the stove gleams. The fruit bowl overflows with apricots, peaches, nectarines, and plums. The spices sit on a special rack, alphabetized. You could tell that many an apple pie has cooled in that open window with the sunshine-yellow eyelet curtains—which match the tablecloth—fluttering in the soft, summertime breeze. Even ardent non-cooks might want to test out a new recipe, or twelve, in this particular kitchen.

Emily arranges the food—just...so—as if the plates were designed to hold noted works of art, even more noted than her pesto scrambled eggs, chicken sausages with sun-dried tomatoes and feta, and homemade blueberry muffins. She sets the plates on the table, sits, and gently places a yellow cloth napkin in her lap.

"How's the remodeling job going?"

"Fine," comes the answer from behind the paper.

Emily quietly eats her breakfast.

David glances into the living room and spots photographs of a younger Emily and Sam in happier, more vibrant days—which don't appear to be all that long ago. A few years, perhaps. His brows come together, practically forming one line across his angelic face.

"Don't ever let it get to you," Penelope says. "Otherwise you're of no good to them at all."

"He's clearly not the life of her love."

"Love of her life," Penelope corrects him. But then she thinks for a moment. "Actually, I like it better your way."

David glances over at Sam and then at Emily again. "So they don't listen much, huh?"

"More and more humans do, overall. The sad thing is they think things are getting worse and worse. But they're not. There are more and more people on the planet with less and less trouble. But the media feels it's their job to report all the horrific things to and from every corner of the globe. And humans just become addicted to this macabre thrill."

Two calico cats skitter across the scrubbed-to-a-sheen tiles on the kitchen floor. They roll up into a ball together, a ball of fur and paws and tails, as they play. Emily's face relaxes into a serene smile as she watches them. David notices a glow starting to radiate from her eyes.

A grunt from Sam causes the smile and the glow to disappear in an instant. Sam smashes the classifieds into one fist, inhales his meal, and then, after semi-unwrinkling the paper, quickly returns to hiding behind it again.

If he weren't an angel, David would swear that the cats winked at him.

"They did," Angela says. "And no swearing."

Not much privacy on this job! David winks back at the cats and then commences another serious study of Emily. "So, this is my assignment, huh?" He's mostly just talking out loud rather than really asking the question.

"Up close and personal," Penelope answers.

"How hard can it be?"

"Oh, watch out. These humans—especially the ones who look easy—can surprise you."

Emily washes the dishes. As she stares out the window over the sink, her face relaxes into a soft, peaceful repose. David follows her gaze—out past her gardens to fields of wildflowers and mountains in the distance. Sam burps and a tautness returns to Emily's features. David feels his heart expand toward this captivating woman who has obviously set her light meter to less than a quarter of its full potential, her power meter to even less than that.

"At bottom, everything is a choice," Penelope tells him. "Absolutely everything."

CHAPTER 2

As the angel teams for Jack, Lacey, and Ben perform their tasks (watching, whispering, consulting the laptop), Brooke and Henry watch Jack, as well.

By the way, speaking of laptops, you humans have not had them all that long; angels have had them since the Dog Star was a pup. So, you might ask, what exactly are Christopher and Stephanie—and all angels assigned to this particular task—watching on their laptops? Oh, all kinds of things. Intent. Karma. Consciousness. Forgiveness. Increases in awareness. Decreases in awareness. Heart openings. Heart closings. You might also ask why the angels don't already have all the answers and see exactly what's going to happen. Well, as we mentioned a little earlier, the future is always in motion. It can go in any direction at any time. So what the chart-watcher angels are watching for is the most likely outcome given all the factors forthcoming in any given moment. But any factor can change—seven billion times over—in any second. That makes for a lot of possibilities! Far too many to track in the mind, even an angel's mind.

Jack and Ben are still hard at work on their dinosaur while Lacey is still hard at work becoming one with the couch.

"The mall is open, but nobody's shopping," Henry whispers to Brooke, referring to Lacey. Brooke is about to respond when an infant cries in another room.

Ben jumps up, causing the dinosaur to fall apart. "Let me go see Chelsea. I want to be alone with her." He runs from the room.

Lacey grunts and starts to lift herself off the couch, completely disgusted at being interrupted in her television staring—we can't even say in all honesty that she was watching it; she was just staring blankly in its direction. After all, if audiences slip into a trance, they're more susceptible, more subject to suggestion, and more prone to filling their overstuffed homes with even more things they don't need. That keeps the advertisers very happy.

"Why is he so insistent on that?" Lacey barks. "He's been like that ever since she was born."

Jack shrugs. "Maybe we should finally let him be with her, but watch him from the hallway."

Jack and Lacey tiptoe down the hallway and peer into the baby's room, where they find Ben leaning his head against the slats of his sister's crib. She has quieted down and is looking intently at her brother. Her three angels are performing their routine: whispering, computing, watching.

In what looks to her parents like the typical baby's head-jerking look-about, Chelsea looks at her angels, at Ben's angels, and then back at her brother. Her room is void of the otherwise ubiquitous piles of who-knows-what and is the cleanest room in the house. Snow White and the Seven Dwarfs parade across one of her bright, peach-colored walls—the painted characters a gift from an artistic coworker of Jack's.

Ben turns to his parents. "I want to talk to her—without you here. Please let me talk to her."

"Okay, big guy," Jack encourages him, "go ahead. You talk to her." Jack pulls a chair over to the crib for Ben to climb onto.

"You can't stay," Ben tells him.

"Okay, we're going."

Jack and Lacey leave, but they stand right outside Chelsea's room, listening.

Ben climbs up on the chair and looks down at his sister. "Can you see them? Can you tell me if they're still here? Please? I don't see them any more."

Tears spring into Jack's eyes, and for a moment he's too stunned to move. Lacey is stunned, too, but for a different reason. She bursts into the nursery.

"Ben, you get down from there. What nonsense are you talking about?" She pushes Ben out of the room and picks up the baby, who was perfectly happy with her brother beside her, but lets out a huge yowl at the rude disruption.

As Ben runs by, tears streaming, Jack grabs him and holds him in a long, close hug. Both of their sets of angels are very moved, very touched by the scene, and they clasp hands with each other.

Henry smiles at Brooke. "So you can see why you've been chosen to be his fourth. He's ready. Are you ready?"

Brooke nods.

Henry points to Ben. "And you can see that he will probably need his fourth angel soon. And perhaps even the baby, too. If a parent is getting it, the children can get it even faster."

Brooke smiles. "That's wonderful."

"Very well," Henry says. "Check in whenever you want to. And not to worry—you really can't get it wrong. Nothing is ever a failure. Nothing is ever, ever a wasted experience for them. Besides, you're in good hands."

The angel teams for Jack and Ben smile at Brooke as Henry leaves. All seven angels watch happily while Jack continues to hold Ben very close to him.

David and Penelope stand alongside Emily's angel team, watching Emily clean her house. Stephanie computes, Jasper whispers, and Angela watches carefully. Actually, the house is already immaculate; what Emily's doing could be called *polishing* her house—which could easily be photographed for a featured spread in a magazine dedicated to comfy, cozy, and classy high-country living. Two oversized, overstuffed sage-green sofas sit facing each other on either side of a large fireplace. Nubbly, hand-woven, darker green throws are gently draped across the backs of both sofas. Between the sofas, a thick, large, round coffee table—a slab taken directly from the middle of an oak tree—commands the space. The table's legs are hewn from the branches of that same tree. The whole array sits on a large green-and-white braided rag rug, which looks like it was made by somebody's great-grandmother while she wiled away more than a few cold winter nights in her little house on the prairie. And that's exactly who made it, and that's exactly where she was.

"You are so loved," Jasper whispers. "You are a blessing. You have so much to give the world. Thank you for all that you do."

Emily looks over toward the group as if she hears something and then, somewhat perplexed, returns to her chores.

Joyfully puzzled, the angels look at each other as if to ask, "Did she just hear us?" They then return to their angelic assignments.

"Can any of them see us?" David asks Penelope.

"Some can. Depends on what they want to see. Almost all babies and old people near their final hours can see us. In both cases, you can see their eyes darting around the room. The veils are very thin at the start and end of life here."

They watch Emily for a few moments. After she finishes dusting the two high-backed rocking chairs that face each other in front of a bay window, she puts her hand over her heart and stares out at her front garden. The soft peacefulness returns to her face.

"She'll be getting it soon," Penelope says. "And whenever one of them gets it, that makes it easier for others to get it, too. It's like a cupful of popcorn in the skillet. There's a pop over here, then another one over there. Pretty soon the whole shebang is popping."

David smiles at the thought.

"Ready?" Penelope asks.

"Sure."

Penelope points to the angel team. "They'll take good care of you. And don't worry. You can't mess it up. Impossible." She disappears.

Sam walks in the kitchen door, and Emily's demeanor and energy instantly shift. Even her breathing turns shallow and panicky.

"Forgot something," Sam mumbles. He disappears up the stairs and then reappears a moment later.

"Bye," Emily says to the slammed door. She shuts her eyes; after a moment or so, her demeanor and energy start to return to something resembling deep and thoughtful. David looks at the other three angels in confusion.

"Why is she bothering with him, you ask?" Angela chuckles. "Every human is allowed a warm-up marriage. Maybe two."

"The warm-up usually doesn't go on for half a decade, however," Stephanie states. "Or it shouldn't, at any rate."

Emily opens her eyes and suddenly lets out a long, huge wail. Remember Lucy Ricardo? This is even worse. David covers his ears and looks at the other angels in sheer shock.

Angela pats him on the back. "Don't worry. You'll get used to it."

"I thought she's a fairly advanced being," David wheezes. "She'd have to be, to get a fourth angel."

"She is. Doesn't mean she's always quiet about it."

Emily wails even louder. She plops into one of the rocking chairs.

"The clashing of the worlds, high and low, can create turbulence in them," Stephanie informs David. "Lots of it."

"Makes for a very interesting, if bumpy, ride," Angela smiles. "For all of us."

"Great," David grimaces.

The angels settle in around Emily as her wails subside. A calm seems to descend upon the room.

Stephanie nudges David. "Oh, no you don't."

"What?"

"Think it's all calm and peaceful in there, too." She pulls up a dial on her laptop. "This is her inner mind-chatter." With her mouse, she clicks the on button. (The computer-watcher angels can use a finger on the screen, too—whichever method they prefer.)

David cringes as the sound of Emily's inner thoughts scrambling all over each other fills the room:

"How can I—When will he—What will I—If only I could—If only he could—When will I—Didn't I say I wouldn't put up with this any more? In all my life—Wonder if I could—shouldn't be like this—"

David backs away from her as if away from a basket teeming with hungry, angry, buzzing bees. On steroids. On a loudspeaker. At a stadium concert. And that was only a fraction of her thoughts—a fraction of thoughts for one second! We could go on for pages and pages and that would only be a few seconds of what goes through her mind.

"How does she live in that thing?" That katzenjammer in her head has to be far worse than the minds of other humans, he thinks. In fact, it has to be worse than if every single thought of every single human on the whole planet could be put together. Okay, maybe not, but gadzooks!

"No one said this was easy," Angela laughs.

"No. No one said that."

"There's a reason for that."

"Great."

Brooke looks over the assortment of monitors on the team's desk in the gargantuan angelic hall. The upper-left monitor shows Jack sleeping next to Lacey. Blake watches carefully, Christopher computes, and Sapphire whispers into her microphone, "You are so loved. You are a blessing. You are so loved. Thank you for all that you do."

On one monitor is a review of Jack's day:

Jack arrives at his office, which appears to be an advertising agency, and immediately has a run-in with his boss, Dick.

Jack absently stares out his office window at the Los Angeles skyline. The clock reads 11:45.

As the sun shines in the conference room, making it stifling hot despite the air conditioning, Jack pretends to be excited as a coworker pitches an ad campaign to a very stuffy, very displeased client.

Jack arrives home. He joyfully picks up the children and plants numerous kisses on their faces amidst Ben's giggling and Chelsea's happy gurgling. Lacey drops onto the couch.

Jack plays with the kids while Lacey stares at the TV.

He finishes putting Chelsea's pajamas on her and gently places her in her crib.

Snuggled together in a small bed, the father reads a book to an enraptured son.

The clock on the wall reads 9:30 as Jack runs on a treadmill at a practically empty fitness club.

He climbs into bed, ignores Lacey's overture, turns his back to her, and closes his eyes.

Brooke notices that even more piles of the who-knows-what, more than any other room, have made it into the bedroom. She turns a dial back to a shot of Jack in his office, which is spotless—a far cry from the way his home is kept. But, Brooke figures, he's probably just given up there, just like he's given up on just about everything...except for his kids. At least he exercises. She lets out a big sigh.

"Sometimes they have to make it get worse before they let it get better," Blake tells her.

On the monitor showing Jack sleeping, little blips of his dreams flash over his head:

As Jack finishes delivering a speech in a large auditorium, the crowd gives him a standing ovation.

Jack and Lacey fight in their bedroom.

Jack frowns in his sleep and moves farther away from his wife.

Jack tosses a baseball to Ben, several years older, who swings his bat and solidly hits the ball.

A smile crosses Jack's face as he sleeps.

A compassionate smile crosses Brooke's face as she watches Jack smile. Without her realizing it, a big smile spreads across Blake's face as he watches her.

Then she sighs again.

"I've been expecting you," Henry says, without looking up, before Brooke's hand even knocks on his open door. "This is not an easy job you signed up for." He finishes the angelwork (well, he wouldn't have paperwork, would he?) on his desk. He waves her into his office, where she drops down onto the cushiest white sofa you ever did see. "My new fourth angels always come back the first night and then not again for eleven weeks. Always. Very strange."

Brooke gives an angelic version of a harrumph. "He obviously adores his children, but he's not happy with his wife and his job and maybe some other things in his life. Why doesn't he just do something about it?"

"There are two main ideas that these humans have to get," Henry explains. "First, get clear. That's ninety-nine percent of it—knowing what it is they want, fer cryin' out loud."

"How are they supposed to know what they want?"

"They have to shut the Heaven up and listen, that's how."

"To us?"

"To us, to themselves. They actually know. They just forget that they know. They go to sleep when they go to Earth and the whole point is to wake up. And to do that they have to check in—frequently and often."

"How?"

"Taking a walk on the beach or in the woods, climbing a mountain, chanting 'Om' on a zafu, whatever. Just by sitting still. Without turning on the radio, TV, MP3 player, cell phone, or whatever else they use to fill up their minds. There's nothing wrong with those things, but humans need a few minutes of silence here and there."

"Doesn't sound hard."

"It isn't. Except they make it hard."

As Stephanie computes, Jasper whispers, and Angela watches, David consults the numerous monitors. On the upper-left monitor, he can see Emily sleeping in a grand four-poster bed. Her bedroom decor is the same as downstairs; the same great-grandmother obviously had enough time on her hands to make a patchwork quilt that adorns the wall, crochet a bedcover, and braid two more rag rugs that warm up the hardwood floor. A bouquet of roses from Emily's garden sits in a white pitcher on her nightstand. Two floral paintings hang on the wall over the bed.

On another monitor is her day-in-review:

Cleaning finished, Emily grabs her purse and leaves the house.

*She drives her red Prius along some winding moun-
tain roads to the bustling center of her little town. She
smiles at a couple of youngish children and their mother
as they sip elaborate, chocolate-drizzled, frothy coffee
drinks—minus the coffee—in front of the town's old-
fashioned-ice-cream-parlor-recently-renovated-to-be-way-
hip-coffee-joint-too place.*

*Emily enters a charming flower shop where she re-
ceives a warm welcome from Marion, the shop's owner, a
radiant woman in her mid-sixties. Marion hands Emily
her paycheck as she prepares to start her workday.*

*Emily holds her mother's hand as the two women sit
in the high-backed rocking chairs. They sip iced tea, relishing each other's company as well as the late afternoon sunshine.*

*Emily finishes brushing her teeth and then stares at
her reflection as she brushes out her hair, which, re-
leased from the braid, cascades down her back in long,
luscious waves.*

*At the sound of Sam's footstep on the front porch,
Emily, upstairs in bed, quickly drops the book she was
reading, turns off the light, and pretends to be asleep.*

David sighs. He looks back to the monitor that
shows Emily sleeping. The contents of a dream appear
in a flash over her head:

*Emily holds her arms out to a couple of very young
children. The three laugh together; in a split second, they
are several years older.*

David starts to look at another monitor, but does a
double take as Emily's next dream starts.

*Against a backdrop of a crimson sun setting over a
cerulean sea, Emily kisses a man that is not Sam.*

The dream evaporates as Emily startles herself
awake. Her angel team instantly transports to her bedroom. Emily, still flustered by her dream, glances over
at her husband, recoiling as a huge snore erupts from

him. She rolls onto her side, facing away from him, and stares into the darkness for a while. Her angels watch her closely, plus Jasper does his whispering. Finally, Emily's eyes shut, and as she drifts off to sleep again, they disappear from her room and reappear back in the giant hall. They take their seats around the desk again, attentive to their assignments.

After several minutes of Emily-sleeping surveillance, David notices the menu along the top of that monitor. He clicks on the drop-down menu under the "Dream Implant" button. He moves the cursor back and forth between "Dreamweaving," "Ultimate Wake Up," and "Special Programming Options."

He jumps as Angela taps him on the shoulder.

"You can't interfere too much, my friend, much as you may want to. We can talk to them and make suggestions all we want, according to the direction they give us from down there and according to the Big Boss. But no special programming. You didn't sign up for this job because it was easy, you know."

"Why are these options here then?"

"For very extreme cases, which you don't have."

David sighs and watches Emily sleep some more before turning back to Angela. "The Big Boss?"

"You'll meet the Big Boss someday," she smiles. "It's not quite time yet."

"Yes, I know," Penelope says, without looking up from her angelwork, before her new angel's hand even knocks on her open door. "It's the hardest job in creation, getting these humans to listen—to what *they* want, which is all that we're here to give them." A dejected David plunks down in the chair in front of her desk as she continues. "You'd think they'd make it easier for themselves...and us."

Henry and Brooke wander back to the desk where the other three members of Jack's angel team diligently tend to their tasks. Brooke watches the dream blips as Jack sleeps. His dreams are fun little snippets of fun things:

Sitting in a bar on an exotic tropical beach, Jack takes the little umbrella out of a piña colada. Attempting to look very serious, he tucks it behind his ear, much to the delight and amusement of a woman sitting next to him.

He strides into Dick's office and hands him a letter of resignation.

Jack and the woman from the tropical-beach dream stroll hand in hand along the Seine in Paris.

Brooke throws her hands up. "He could do any of those things," she cries to Henry. "He doesn't have to do them just in his dreams."

"Well, dreams are where they start."

"He could do all that tomorrow. Just do it. Just say yes." Henry looks at her. "Those clichés don't always travel across the galaxies and stay in their natural state," she mutters.

"Well," Henry says, "Earth can be viewed as a school. Humans can't go from kindergarten to a doctorate program overnight. But they do have to discover what they truly want."

Brooke is too flummoxed even to ask any questions. She watches Jack play with Chelsea in his dream.

"Here, you think you have problems with him? Get a load of this one." He takes Brooke's arm. She finds herself floating through the ceiling of a cramped studio apartment as a woman, about thirty or so, prepares her pre-dawn breakfast. With typical love and diligence, her angel team performs its assignments around her.

"No elevator?"

"No, hon, once you've been downloaded to Earth, you don't have to keep being downloaded. You can beam yourself. That's how you arrived back at the hall when Jack fell asleep."

"Oh, right. Of course." Brooke giggles at her own absentmindedness.

They watch the woman as she flips her frying egg to make it easy-over.

"I want to move to France," she announces to the air in a thick New York accent. Unbeknownst to her, the air hears her—or at least her team of angels, which fills the air around her, hears her. Her angels start moving to the left—computing, affirming, and figuring how to assist her in moving to France.

The woman grabs her freshly popped toast and butters it. "No, I want to stay here and find a husband." Again, the air, in the form of her angel team, responds; they start moving to the right—computing, affirming, and figuring how to assist her in finding a husband and continuing to live in New York City.

"No, I want to live the wild-and-crazy life and have lots of lovers all over the world." Her very obedient angels start moving to the left again.

"No, I want a house in the country. And a horse." Her angels start moving to the right again.

The woman stares at the breakfast she has set on the table. "No—oh, I don't know." After this last statement, her angels stand around her, waving their fists in the air.

"Waddya want?" the team leader demands. "Make up your mind!"

"Good thing we have infinite energy, eh?" Henry questions.

"What was the second thing?" Brooke asks him.

"Second thing?"

"You said there were two things humans have to do. First, be clear."

"Second," Penelope announces to David, "don't give up before the miracle happens!"

"How are they supposed to know it's on its way or almost here or whatever?" David wonders.

"By stopping that incessant yammering they do inside their heads. That would certainly help. They all get all kinds of signals and hints and nudges, but do you think they listen?"

David and Penelope walk back to the team's desk. They look at the upper-left monitor and watch Emily sleep for a little bit.

"Sleep was certainly a great invention to get them to shut the Heaven up," Penelope snipes. "They have to reboot sometime."

David isn't quite sure what to make of all this.

"Here, let me show you something." She takes him by the hand, and he suddenly finds himself on a picturesque New England beach at sunrise. David spies a middle-aged man walking his dog at the water's edge, angel team in tow.

"Okay, what's with him?" David asks.

"First he was looking for another job, and his angels were setting up interviews for him. Then he up and quits his job and goes on a joyride to Florida. He stayed there, found a job, and then asked for his life's partner. They set one up for him—took a year—and the day before he was supposed to meet her on an escalator in the mall, he up and moved here. He started out in Ohio."

"Wow."

"There's nothing wrong with doing all that," Penelope says, "but if they want things, they have to give us a little time, especially when they're not exactly crystal clear. Then they wonder what in the world is wrong with them—'why can't I find a partner,' 'why am I still in this same dead-end job,' things like that."

"Can't his angels foresee what he would be doing and arrange, oh, say the job in Florida or the partner here in Massachusetts?"

"Well, like I told you, the future is constantly moving. It can change at any time. Instantly. We have to go by what they're thinking in the moment. And what state they're in—literally as well as figuratively."

They watch the man as he lets out a very long, very slow exhale, looking out over the ocean.

"He keeps getting it all practically delivered to him, wrapped up with a bow. But he throws it all away, just because he's impatient and won't stay in one place long enough to listen."

The dog jumps up on her human, breaking his reverie, and the man throws a stick into the water for her. David can feel the man's heart opening.

"At least he has a great dog."

"The one thing he'd let us arrange for him."

Penelope and David reappear in her office.

"It doesn't have to be hard," Penelope tells him. "When they're in the flow of what they're supposed to be doing, it's easier than trying to force themselves to do something they're not supposed to be doing. Challenges may come up, but that's just making jewels."

"How's that again?"

"Irritating sand becomes a lustrous pearl. Pressure forms a dazzling diamond."

David nods. Penelope motions toward the door with her head. As he leaves her office, he glances back and notices that she's returned to her angelwork, but she's smiling and nodding her head.

CHAPTER 3

After Henry leaves, Brooke watches the monitor that shows Jack sleeping, paying special attention to his dream blips.

Jack kisses his wife. To the Jack-in-the-dreamstalk's great joy, he discovers that Lacey has turned into another woman, and he quickly takes the kiss to a much more exuberant level. A smile crosses Jack's sleeping face. *In the dream, he takes the woman in his arms, and they move in a slow dance, which ends in a dip with an even more exuberant kiss.*

A smile crosses Brooke's face. So passion is there—if only in his dreams. Unbeknownst to her, smiles cross the faces of the other three angels, as well. And they weren't just smiling about Jack.

On the monitor, the angels notice a sleeping Sam throw his arm over Emily, waking her up. The angels disappear from the office...

...and reappear in the bedroom. Emily very carefully disentangles herself from Sam's headlock and glances at the clock. 5:30. In super-stealth mode, she slips out of bed, reaches for her robe and slippers, and leaves the room.

Downstairs in the kitchen, Emily turns on the burner under the kettle. As she waits for the water to boil, she stares out the window. A peaceful, serene air settles over her entire being.

A mug of steaming tea in hand, Emily sits down in one of the rocking chairs by the window in the living room. She gazes out at the iridescent sky to see the red, coral, yellow, and orange clouds announcing the coming sunrise and the later rainfall. She shuts her eyes in meditation. A moment later, a creak in the floorboard just over her head brings her to a slump as her deeply peaceful demeanor becomes deeply annoyed, deeply disheartened, deeply sad.

"Emily, my dear," Angela says, "you've given it another chance. And another chance. And another. It's clearly not working." She motions for David to talk to their human.

"Emily, it sure doesn't have to be like this." He looks back at Angela, who gestures for him to continue. "Emily, you're supposed to be happy. You're of much greater service to everyone if you're happy, plus it makes the Earth journey a lot more fun." David looks at Angela again, who nods, impressed. "For all of us."

"She'll get it," Angela assures him. "Someday. She has eternity."

"Great."

Jack slumps lower and lower in his seat as his car gets closer and closer to his house. Brooke wonders how he can even see over the steering wheel, he's slumping so much. His old, red Honda has seen better days, but it's spotless, too, like his office. The air inside it seems oppressively sad, though. Well, that'd make sense, she figures; he's in the car for at least two hours a day, most days. It's bound to pick up his state of being. If humans only knew how big they are, she sighs to herself. And how much they affect. And—

"Jack," Blake says, "buddy boy, bubbala, kiddo, waddya doing? When are you going to find yourself a new playing field? I mean, no matter what the field, it's still the same game you play within yourself, but why play at a sub-minor field when you can play at Wrigley? Or Dodger? Or Fenway?"

Blake motions to Brooke to talk to him.

"Jack, you're supposed to be happy here in this lifetime," Brooke tells him. Brooke looks at her superior, who signals for her to continue. "Jack, we want this to happen now. As soon as possible." Brooke looks back at Blake again, who nods, then motions for her to keep going. "Well, in divine ASAP, at any rate."

Blake takes another turn. "Jack, you know, if you don't listen to us, your guidance, life has to get through to you via more drastic and extreme measures."

Jack just drives, oblivious. He pulls into his driveway. He slumps even lower in his seat—good thing he doesn't have to see over that steering wheel anymore—as he turns off the engine. Once outside the car, he takes a moment to square his shoulders. But they cave in again as soon as he heads toward his house, angels close behind.

"He's given up," Brooke moans.

"A lot of 'em do," Blake says.

"He's just going to settle, make do."

"A lot of 'em do."

"What about his kids? They bring him such joy."

"Even they can't lift up what seems to be emerging as the overarching game plan of his life."

"Jack, this is not what you came here for!" Brooke practically tugs him on the arm, but of course he can't feel it.

"None of 'em are. But some give up."

"But he's supposed to be an advanced being!"

Blake wheezes. "Sometimes they're the hardest!"

Sapphire suddenly raises her whispering to normal voice range. "You are beautiful. You are a blessing. Thank you for coming here." Brooke and Blake look at her in surprise as her voice becomes even louder. "Jack, you are so loved. You are a miracle. Thank you for all that you do."

Christopher holds his laptop up so they can see its report. Brooke puts her hand over her face.

"Oh, wow," Blake says, shaking his head. "Well, if he'da just listened to us in the first place, fer the love of Life—"

Jack opens the front door. The assembly of human and angels hears muffled voices and what sounds like rats scurrying down the hall. Jack walks into the bedroom just in time to see Dick, buck naked, dive into the closet. Lacey, after swiftly wrapping her robe around her, puts her hand over her mouth in some semblance of regret—although clearly not for doing what she was doing, but that she got caught doing what she was doing. After taking a moment to recover from his shock,

Jack opens the closet door. Dick waves at him, sheepishly. Kind of.

Jack turns to Lacey. "It's not like I don't come home every single day at this time."

Dick and Lacey look at each other, then back at Jack.

"Ah. That was the idea."

No response.

"The closet thing supposed to make me feel better, like you're at least a little sorry?"

No response.

"Where are the kids?"

Lacey speaks through her hand, still pressed to her mouth. "My mother's."

As Jack drives, his angels hang not just around but on and all over his seat.

"Just feel it all—get it out," Blake says. "And then send her love, son."

"You mean to his wife?" Brooke asks.

Blake nods. "It advances him to do that, especially in a time like this. Plus, whatever he sends out, he gets back exponentially."

"Uh, okay."

"It's a cause-and-effect universe," Blake explains. "Whatever you give, you get. And if you're looking for more of something, like love, like money, whatever, then give more of something, like love, like money, whatever. It's a law, just like gravity."

"This seems like hardly the time to be sending and getting more love."

"This is the best time."

Ben bounces up and down at the sight of his father in the doorway. "Daddy! Daddy!"

Jack gives him a hug and then reaches to take the baby from his mother-in-law's arms. "Thanks for taking care of them, Irene."

"You're welcome." Irene looks out at the car, frowning. "What happened to Lacey? I thought she was going to pick them up."

"She had something unexpected pop up. Wait, cancel that—it was expected."

Jack takes Ben's hand and walks him to the car, while balancing Chelsea on his hip. Once both children are in their car seats, Ben cries out, "Where are we going, Daddy?"

"Anywhere you want to go, big guy. You name it."

"Oh, boy!"

Jack holds Ben's hand while pushing Chelsea's carriage with his other hand as they meander down the sidewalk alongside the beach. Jack picks Ben up and places him on the wall separating the sidewalk from the sand. Even young Ben is enthralled by the resplendence of the sun setting over the ocean and is quiet for a few moments.

"I wish we could do this every day, Daddy."

"Me, too."

Clink! Emily and her mother, Barbara, settled in the rocking chairs, touch their glasses of homemade lemonade together, toasting to—oh, nothing in particular. They just like to bring a touch of special to any and every moment they spend together. And that lemonade really is homemade—organic Meyer lemons, spring water, organic maple syrup.

Barbara's refined beauty belies over seven decades spent on a farm. Her white hair lights up her unlined face. The three angels clustered around her are devoted to their tasks, although Barbara clearly is not a hardship post—at least not at this point in her life. She had her day.

The two women look out at the yard, still somewhat soggy from the morning's rainfall. The flower beds extend all the way around the house and down the pathway leading to the guest cottage. When Emily's father died and her mother sold the farm, she came to stay for a while. Since that was a few years ago now, her guest status has morphed into resident status.

Near Barbara's cottage is an enormous pile of logs, neatly stacked. Oh, you might think big, burly, once-hunky-now-kinda-chunky Sam would have been the one to split those logs, but no, that's one of the many, many ways Emily stays so fit. She also mowed the yard, hoed the vegetable garden, and, well, just about everything else related to the house and yard. Cars, too. She could also catch and cook supper over an open fire, if needed. So she's really not as frail as she likes to pretend.

"Mom, why don't you get married again?"

"Trying to get rid of me?"

"Not in a million years."

"I had the best husband in the world. There was no topping him. No way, no how."

"Wish I could've inherited that from you."

"I do, too."

"Don't start."

"You started it!"

"Oh. Yeah, I guess I did." Emily gulps the rest of her lemonade. "Time to go to work."

"There goes the great escape artist. Except from her own marriage."

"Oh, Mom!"

As she parks her car, Emily spots a man emerging from the flower shop with a dozen roses. At first, her expression registers something like envy—wistful envy—but a slow smile starts to appear.

David tries to listen in on her thoughts, but for once it's rather quiet in there, except for a faint "Yes." He looks at Angela, somewhat baffled.

"She knows the last thing you do when you want something is begrudge someone else for having it. Their having it means that it's available for everyone, not that there's less for everyone."

David nods in agreement, but then stops short, shaking his head at her and raising his hands in the universal gesture of massive befuddlement.

"I know," Angela chuckles. "These humans are something else. This idea goes up, that idea goes down, one lesson learned, another forgotten. And sometimes when they're finally—finally!—getting it all together, that's when everything really falls apart. Can't let 'em get to you."

Ching! The bells on the door announce Emily's arrival, and Marion greets her with a hug. David looks around the shop to see where the extra light is coming from, because Marion is far more illuminated than the overcast afternoon would allow. She radiates a special light, but even that is faint compared to the light of her constant smile. Marion has four angels, who all happen to be meditating. No whispering or watching required here. On occasion, the chart-watching angel opens an eye to glance at his laptop, but then returns to his meditation.

Her angel team leader is an avuncular gentleman with a big handlebar mustache. He opens one eye and spots David. "Albert."

David shakes the hand that Albert has extended to him. (Yes, angels like that handshaking habit, too.) "David." Albert returns to his meditation.

"And how are you on this lovely day?" Marion asks Emily.

Emily scrunches her face at her boss—immediately prior to the question, the skies opened up.

"Okay, yes, it's a little wet, maybe. But it's still lovely." Marion's normal speaking voice is melodic, almost like singing. "The frogs and flowers are happy." She returns to her project of snipping the ends of the stems of a dozen glorious, red roses. Baby's breath and greens lie on the thick wooden table waiting to be added to the arrangement. The two women are surrounded by a sea of roses, daffodils, and tulips among many, many other types of flowers. The air inside the little store is thick with moisture and the scent of dirt and life in full bloom.

Emily tucks her purse into the cabinet under the cash register and grabs a broom and dustpan to dispose of the morning's snippings. Judging from the copious piles of tiny green stalks on the floor, housekeeping is not Marion's primary care, nor her hundredth. And her plants, who (yes, who) are among the top beings on her priority list, are very happy about that.

Emily sweeps with far more vigor than the chore calls for. Marion snips an inch off of the stem of the rose destined to be the star of this little rose party. She then snips two inches off of the stems of the roses that will surround the center flower. Emily catches them with the dustpan before they even hit the floor.

"Your mom doing okay?" Marion gently queries.

Emily nods. More snipping, more catching. She grabs a cloth to dust the vases on the shelves.

"And how are things with Sam?" comes another soft inquiry.

Emily doesn't answer.

"I was married to potential for a long time. Doesn't compare to the real thing."

Emily knocks a vase over, but catches it before it hits the floor. "He could be so much more than he is!"

"Not all beings feel obliged to use all that they come in with."

Emily lets out a long, long wail. While Emily's angels cover their ears, Marion calmly hands her a box of tissues.

Ching! The tinkling of the bells on the front door alerts them that they have a customer. A stocky woman in her mid-forties, dressed in business attire, leans on the counter. She might usually sport a more imposing posture in most places, but after stealing a glance at the two women, she quickly scans the store before casting her gaze to the floor.

"Good afternoon," Marion says, all smiles and radiance. "Are you looking for something in particular?"

The woman is not quite sure what to say. "Well, not flowers. A friend told me about you. I just drove all the way from Seattle. Perhaps I should have called, but—"

"What is it? Cancer?" Marion's obvious love and reverence for the newcomer softens the bluntness of the question.

The woman nods, blinking away tears.

"Welcome." Marion locks the front door and flips the "Open" sign around to display the words "Back at" over a clock, which she arranges to reveal that they'll be back in a couple of hours. Emily, completely shifted from caterwauling mode, motions the visitor toward the back of the shop.

"What's your name?" she asks.

"Veronica."

Marion and Emily lead Veronica out the back door, across an enchanting patio area chock-full of statues and bubbling fountains with majestic evergreens standing in silent, sacred sentry around the perimeter. For those that might not know, the trees are on your side. They hear everything you say. They celebrate your wins; they mourn your losses along with you. As Penelope said when David first arrived on Earth, "Powerful beings, those trees."

The three women step into a one-room cottage on the far end of the property. More statues and fountains as well as plants bedeck the room. Artwork and fabrics hang on the walls while rose quartz, jade, and a number of other stones sparkle on the side tables. Soft, soothing music pours from hidden speakers. The fragrance of several flower arrangements fills the space, as does a blend of essential oils in a diffuser: rose, myrrh, geranium, patchouli, lemon balm, to name just a few.

The room feels alive—and it is. David observes numerous tiny beings flittering and gliding through the air. If you were to take a photograph of this room, little orbs might appear all over the picture. Most people think those orbs are tricks of the light or the camera; they're not.

And Emily! Who in the cosmos is this stranger? It's like...it's like...well, David tried to think of exactly just what she's suddenly like. Perhaps it's like she just landed in her feet—as if just a moment ago she decided to fully incarnate and take up residence in her body and on the planet. Like she put on an invisible vestment of....assurance. Fortitude. Major mettle.

A massage table stands as the centerpiece of the room. As Marion turns down the sheet and comforter, Veronica kicks off her shoes, then stretches out on the table. Marion covers her while Emily dims the lamps and lights a few candles. Both women raise their hands, holding them parallel over and about one foot higher than Veronica. Light streams from their hands— at least from the angels' vantage point. The humans can't see it, but all three of them can certainly feel it.

"Just let go of whatever's been eating away at you, release any growing resentments," Marion whispers. "Inside and out. Just let them all go."

Veronica starts to speak.

"We don't need to know the history behind it, my dear," Marion says. "This is a brand-new moment. You can decide anything you want from here on out. Just be crystal clear about it."

Marion's angels open their eyes and shoot David a "you-can-see-why-we're-meditating" kind of look. David looks at the rest of his team, motioning with both hands toward Emily.

"All in good time," says Angela.

"But she's—"

"Enjoy it while it lasts," Stephanie snickers.

But, still, judging from this magnificent being before him, David thinks that the good time Angela mentioned can't be far away.

Tears slip down Veronica's face. David watches a black cloud dislodge from her body as the energy emit-from her healers' hands does its work.

About half an hour later, Marion sits down, eyes shut, hands up with palms facing Veronica. Emily continues healing, swaying in the flow of...grace? She's clearly in an altered state and performing potent work. Oh! You would hardly know it's the same woman as the one who was just sniveling about her husband. Well, you might know it because you have a clue in the serene, peaceful way she gazes out her living room window and at other times here and there. You can tell there's a powerhouse way down inside there—hiding for who only knows what reason.

Well, actually, there is a reason. Powerhouses can get brought down—or, more correctly, people try to bring them down. But true power can never, ever be brought down. It lives in everyone, and it can't be taken away. Sometimes an entire life journey can be about just this one lesson.

After another half an hour or so, Marion rises, and she and Emily finish their labor-of-true-love together. The energy surges, electrifying the room as the two women stand over Veronica for several more minutes, "shining" their hands on her. David beams at the sheer rapture on Emily's face.

They put their hands down. After a few moments of stillness, Veronica stirs. "Ohhhhhhhhhh, I feel so wonderful," she purrs.

"Couldn't she have done this on her own?" David asks Angela.

"Oh, sure, if she was meant to. But they shouldn't do everything alone. What would they need each other for then?"

Emily and Marion walk Veronica back across the garden patio and into the store.

"How much do I owe you?"

"Whatever you'd like to give," Marion says.

"I don't have much now. It's all gone to the other form of medicine. All of it. I'll send more as soon as I can." She hands them a check for fifty dollars and starts to leave. Emily presents her with a bouquet of flowers. Veronica tries to talk, but words cannot escape from her lips.

"It worked," Emily states after Veronica floated out the door.

"It certainly did."

Emily looks pleased, then puzzled. "Why can't I do this with my mother?"

"She hasn't asked you to."

Emily thinks for a moment. "My sister did. Without even knowing what she was asking for. And I gave it to her without even knowing what I was doing."

"Another journey was calling Lisa more."

"She could have stayed."

"She obviously didn't want to."

Emily nods and wipes away a tear.

"You're a vessel for those who want you to be one, those who are called to what you have. And regarding those for whom your energy doesn't work, well, we just don't know to what other places and expeditions they've been called."

Angela smiles at David's raised eyebrows. "Marion's a live one. Literally."

Brooke and Blake watch the monitor that shows Jack sleeping while Christopher consults his laptop and Sapphire whispers into the microphone: "You're a miracle. You're such a blessing. You're so loved. Thank you for all that you are."

Brooke turns to Blake. "Have you ever seen God?"

Blake nods.

"When?"

"Every second of every minute of every hour of every day of every light-year of my existence."

Brooke lets this wash over her. "Huh. Okay. Just wondering. Good to know."

"And I've been around for a very long time," he adds. "And so have you. There's never been a time without any one of us, in one form or another."

Brooke lets this wash over her, as well. She pulls up some information on one of the monitors, studies it, and then addresses the sleeping man. "Oh, Jack, do you remember your agreement? You said you would wake up in this lifetime. It's time to actualize that agreement."

On the screen, she can see the sleeping Lacey accidentally belt Jack in the face. Jack wakes with a start.

Blake chuckles. "Well, that's sure one way to wake him up! Back down we go."

Reassembled in the bedroom, Sapphire continues her whispering and Christopher his computing while the two others stare at Jack as he stares at the ceiling. Very exciting.

Jack looks at the clock, which reads 2:45. He looks over at Lacey.

"Jack," Blake chides, "when I said to send her love, I didn't mean you had to keep doing it on and on, especially so directly!"

"Jack," Brooke pleads, "you're supposed to wake up. Metaphorically, I mean. You can sleep now if you want. In fact, that would be a really good idea."

Blake leans over and bellows in Jack's ear. "Jack, perhaps it's time to leave Lacey."

"Jack," Brooke implores, "there's more for you than this."

Jack looks over at his sleeping, snoring wife and then looks back at the ceiling. He turns on his side, facing away from her.

The clock reads 4:30 as Jack shuts his eyes. The angels wait for a moment before converging at their desk.

"What are we going to do?"

Blake considers Brooke's question. "Hmmmm. He's actually getting more and more awake and aware, believe it or not, but he's not going to leave her. He's still stuck on that old-time religion thing. It worked for humanity for a while, but many haven't moved past it yet."

"Old-time religion?" Brooke huffs. "But this is California, Los Angeles even, not Kansas!"

"There are still enclaves, even here," Blake clarifies. "You're looking at two members of an enclave right now. And you just might be surprised about Kansas, by the way. These two are far more conservative than a bunch there."

"So what can we do? Is there anyone we can send along to entice him out of his marriage?"

"He won't go for that, even if his wife did. He's too noble."

Brooke sighs—well, grunts, really. "He's not leaving her. He's not waking up. He's not following his plan at all."

"Well, they were supposed to come together to birth those two beautiful beings."

"Check. It's done."

Christopher looks up from his computer. "He's certainly not going to leave a baby."

"Well, that's true."

Christopher turns his laptop around to show them what he's been studying. "And his charts show he's still not going to leave her, despite everything."

"What else can we do?"

"Job change? Get fired? The old boss is banging the old wiferoo, so he'd probably want Jack far away from here."

"Nah," Blake says. "Lacey would just go with him. He's her meal ticket."

"Couldn't Dick be, that, too?" Brooke asks.

Christopher keys in some information and studies the results. "No."

"How about—"

"Nah."

"I know, we could—"

"Nah."

Three months later—which might seem like a bit of a while to humans, but not to angels—"How about—"

"Nah."

"Big Boss time?" Christopher asks Blake.

Brooke's eyebrows shoot up.

"Perhaps," Blake says. "Let's give it a little more time."

No one responds to the very obvious question on Brooke's face.

"How about—"

"Nah."

"Okay, Big Boss time," Blake announces. "Brooke, go find something to do somewhere else."

Sam makes a few less-than-graceful moves on top of Emily, who is pretty much doing a great lump-on-a-log imitation. Both of their angel teams meditate with their backs to the couple, giving them privacy.

When Sam finishes, he rolls over. Their angels face them again. A second later, Emily hears a loud snore. Sam's angels disappear to the great office in the sky. In the galaxy, really.

Emily looks at the clock: 12:45. She stares at the ceiling. Long gone is the powerhouse from the flower shop we saw a few months ago; it doesn't look like there's a full-blooded human being residing on the planet, in her body, even in her feet.

All four of her angels start whispering to her—even Stephanie puts down her computer.

"Emily, you'll be fine without him," Angela urges.

"Emily, there's a whole life waiting for you," David adds.

"Emily, this doesn't calculate anymore," Stephanie joins in.

"Emily, you're beautiful, you're a miracle, you are so loved," whispers Jasper. "For God's sake, woman!" No whisper there. If the rest of his team was comprised of humans, they might've gotten whiplash from swiveling their heads so quickly. Jasper quickly returns to his usual whispering. "You are so beautiful. You are such a miracle. You are so loved."

"Let this love show up in your life in a much better way," Angela suggests to her human.

"Just let him go," David pleads with her, as well.

"This really doesn't compute, Emily," Stephanie says. "There's nothing wrong with either of you. It's a matter of incompatible software, that's all. You just don't interface."

"Emily, you are so loved," Jasper whispers. "You are so loved. You are so loved."

A tear slips down Emily's face.

The next morning, Emily stumbles into the shop.

"Good morning. How are you, dear one?"

Emily bursts into tears. The wail isn't far behind. Again, while Emily's angels cover their ears, Marion calmly holds out the box of tissues. "It sometimes needs to get worse before it gets better," she says.

"Hey, she's taking our job!" David laughs.

Three-ten AM. Emily finally falls asleep. Her angels transport back to their desk.

"Alright then, it's time to check in with the Big Boss," Angela proclaims.

"Finally!"

"Not you," Angela says to David. "You wait here. You have to be doing this angel thing for a while before you can do a check-in." She shoos him away.

Somewhat disgruntled, he watches the rest of the team hover around an as-yet-unused (as far as David was concerned, anyway) monitor on the desk. After a little while, Stephanie snaps off the monitor.

"Well?" David tries to hide his annoyance.

"There might be something coming down the cosmic freeway," Angela grins.

"Did you just talk to God?"

"Yes. Just like I do every single time I talk."

CHAPTER 4

Nine-thirty. The book Emily was reading slips from her hands as she falls asleep.

Her angels disappear from her room...

...and appear at their desk.

On the "Human's Ambient Sound" speaker, they hear a dog barking in the distance, which wakes up their charge. Her angels disappear from the great hall...

...and reappear at her bedside. Emily puts her book on her night table, snuggles under her covers, and quickly slips into sleep again.

Her angels disappear from her room...

...and reappear at their desk.

"Great exercise," David says.

But Angela simply stares at the monitor, watching Emily sleep; Jasper whispers; Stephanie computes.

After a while, David stands up, looks around their area of the great hall, and starts to pace. The teams in many of the surrounding cubicles diligently attend to their tasks, while other cubicles are empty because that team's human is still up and about.

David overhears one angel talking to the rest of her group: "I know, you could have this woman's phone line go down and send this repairman over there and on the way, he could run into—"

David roams down the aisle a little more. As he passes an unangeled (yes, well, we can't exactly say un-peopled, can we?) cubicle, David spots a heretofore un-noticed small monitor showing a human being doing her human thing and her angels doing their angelic things. Since David is always away from the desk while he and the team are with Emily, he's never seen that a monitor plays the whole human/angel day in their absence. He leans closer to see what this particular human is up to: she tosses items into her grocery cart and heads a little further down the supermarket aisle. Nothing very monumental here. He straightens up and notices that Angela has stopped watching Emily and instead has her eyes on him.

"Everything's monumental," Angela says.

"Pardon?" He's irritated at himself for slacking on his duties as well as for thinking something he'd rather not have his superior pick up on.

"It's okay."

There she goes again! David strides back to the cu-bicle devoted to Emily. His irritation doubles, then qua-druples onto itself—he's irritated at himself for being irritated, which only increases the irritation. He whis-tles in an attempt to clear his mind.

"That woman at the supermarket is about to have eye contact with a man who appears to be alone, but isn't—his girlfriend is just further down the aisle. The man's attention back to this woman sends his girlfriend into a rage because it's just the very last straw on the camel's back, as humans like to say. But mostly because it's the higher road on her path. She's going to leave him, then meet the man she's going to marry, and together they parent a child who is eventually going to be the President."

She lets David digest the vast implications of a trip to the supermarket. "But the future's always in motion, as Penelope told me," he finally comments.

"Right, but some things, like who's going to be President, are somewhat fixed. They have to be." She lets him think about that for a few moments, too. "Feel like going on a galactic gallivant?"

"Huh?"

"That'd be a 'road trip,' as humans would call it."

"We're allowed to do that?"

"Of course."

"Um, sure."

Angela takes David's arm and the two disappear from the great hall...

...and appear in the heart of Skid Row on New York's Bowery.

Several drunks snore in a doorway. David notices that they shimmer with light. Their computing angels compute, their watching angels watch, and their whispering angels whisper to them: "You are loved. You are a blessing. You are a miracle. You can wake up to the light that you are—any time. You are loved. You are a blessing."

Angela and David watch them for a while, until she taps him on the shoulder and points to one particular man. "Look, he's about to die. You can see his family, his friends, even his dog—they're all lining up to greet him."

David notices that the dying drunk shimmers more than the others and that light beings, including one in a canine shape, hover over him.

"But don't beings move on to their next incarnation, their next phase, whatever that is?" David asks. "How can all of them be waiting for him—and all those beings for all those humans—when they die?"

"It's a hologram," Angela explains. "One piece represents the whole. We're all part of this whole, plus we can be anything at any time, anywhere. So our beloved ex-humans/light beings here can be on to their next phase, whatever that is, and they can be there to greet their loved ones when they pass on and congratulate them for a job well done."

"But this one was a drunk!"

"That was his disguise, yes. We're all drops in the vast ocean of infinity, cleverly disguised as a drunk or an angel or whatever we choose. And just living a life on Earth is a job well done. It's not exactly easy here, you may have noticed."

The drunk slowly opens his eyes. As he notices his three angels sitting around him, he blinks. When they don't disappear—they're really there, he realizes—he tries to sit upright but fails. The computing angel puts away his computer.

"Look, he's about to talk to his angels," Angela says. "He's at the point where he can see between the worlds."

"Am I dying?" the drunk asks his angels.

"Yes, my love," responds an angel. "You are. But it's not an ending. It's a new beginning."

"Anything'd be better than this."

"You did well, my dear," says another angel. "Earth is one of the toughest places in the universe."

"Probably could've done better."

"Yes, perhaps you could have," responds the third angel. "Perhaps next time you will. It's your choice. And it's all good."

Tears roll down the man's face.

"Your family and friends are waiting for you." An angel points to a shaft of light that has appeared overhead, much like a spotlight shining in a theater.

"They hated me!"

"They don't any more."

"I didn't do too well here."

"You evolved your soul. That's all you needed to do."

The drunk leans his head back and slumps as the life force leaves his body. His human-shaped form of light detaches itself from his physical body—hands and feet first, then his head, and then the rest of the light body follows. His light form starts to rise. A chorus of cheers and party sounds—barks, too—erupt from the group of light beings as his light form rises up to meet them.

"Atta boy!"

"Welcome home!"

"Mom! Dad!" the man cries. He throws his arms around them, but not very successfully. He tries again, and this time his arms pass through them a little less rapidly. Third time's a charm: becoming accustomed to his arms of light, he slowly wraps them around his parents. After a few moments relishing the reconnection, he turns to the next being in the receiving line. "You! You sank my business! You took my entire life away from me! You turned me into a drunk! No—oh my God!" he hoots. "That was *you*?" After a couple of pats on the back that pass right through his former nemesis, the third pat meets its target. "That was you all along? Holy moly, you sure had me going!"

The shouts of welcome and greeting slowly start to fade up and away. The dog barks more raucously.

"Hey Buddy—how ya doin' ole pal? It's been such a long, long time!"

Angela and David smile at each other.

"Quite a homecoming," David says.

"Oh, yes. They all get something like that."

"What's next for him? What's next for his angels?"

"Whatever they want, whatever they choose." Angela takes David's arm and they disappear...

...and appear in a stately mansion overlooking a beach. The sun is setting over the Pacific—reds and oranges and yellows glow in bright bands of colors on the clouds. But the very genteel-looking, golden-aged man and woman keep their eyes glued to the television, martini glasses in hand.

David shifts about, waiting for something to happen, but the couple just stares at the high-def widescreen. After a bit, it dawns on him that they're not even seeing what they're watching. "No one's home!"

"No, no one's home," Angela concurs.

"Plus, they're each a drunk, too, just like the other fellow."

"Oh, these humans are so clever. Even their disguises can take so many interesting disguises."

Angela and David watch them for a while longer until Angela takes David's arm and they disappear....

...and appear in a cold, dark room. David sees four angels holding the hands—two angels holding each hand—of a young woman as a man forces himself on her. Three men lounge in chairs along the wall, waiting to take a turn.

The three angels of the rapist shout to him, "Stop! Please! You can do better than this! You are here to be a blessing! You are loved!"

David looks around him in complete shock and disbelief. "What...in...creation......?"

The three angels of the last man in line whisper to him. "You are a blessing. You are loved. You are here to share love. Please wake up. You can do so much good with your life."

The man, a younger, less rough version of the other men, slowly stands up and slips out the door. His angels clasp hands, dance, and hug each other as they follow him out.

"He heard them," David smiles.

"Yes, at some level."

David watches the woman again. While her rapist is still in action, her eyes are fixed on the ceiling. Her angels speak to her: "You are loved. You are strong. You will find a better life and teach others to be strong. And you'll do it so well because you've had to be so strong, dear one. They'll look up to you because you've truly had to follow the road of finding your inner strength. You are so loved. You are so strong."

The heartbreaking anguish on the woman's face transforms into resolve. Her eyes follow the pattern of the cracks in the ceiling as if she's looking for a specific symbol; the search distances her mind and spirit from her physical circumstances. David notices that the darkness of the trauma in and on her body is easing, even though her attacker's motions have intensified.

"In answer to your question," Angela says, "it's one of the greatest mysteries in creation, the evil that humans can do to each other. Sometimes it's for greater strength. Sometimes it's for greater contrast. Sometimes, well, God only knows, literally. Sometimes it's just plain unbelievable."

They float out of the dingy apartment building and float higher and higher off the ground. A snowcapped mountain range glistens in the distance, and David notices that the highway signs are not in English.

"But you must respect her—you must respect every single one of them—as a cocreator of her journey, as cocreators of all of their journeys," Angela states. "She is not a victim. She is evolving her soul. We don't know what these beings have chosen to work on in any particular incarnation."

"You and I—any angel—could look it up on their charts."

"Well, of course. But just looking at a situation from the outside, at the human level, often won't tell you very much. But life is always moving toward a higher good. It's not happening *to* them; it's happening *for* them."

"Well, but just because others don't know that either, it doesn't mean they shouldn't stop an injustice from happening."

"You're right," Angela agrees. "Being awake and aware and not doing anything about an injustice is far, far worse than being asleep and perpetuating the injustice."

She takes David by the arm...

...and they float over a tarmac in the middle of a desert. Two men approach a plane filled with food and medical supplies. After a moment of intense negotiation with the pilot, they hand him some money.

All three have three angels who are talking to them nonstop: "Please share this wealth. Please give it to the hungry. You are loved. You are a blessing. You can do better than this. Please awaken to your true nature. Please discover your higher destiny. You are loved."

The men signal to a crew to unload the plane. Once the plane is empty, the pilot boards it.

The pilot's angels try to appeal to him. "You are loved. You are a blessing. You have great things to do. There is more to life than money."

"You can't do anything in this godforsaken place without money, and there's no other way to get any!" the pilot screams to the windshield of his plane.

After a moment of stunned silence, the angels high five and hug each other.

"He heard them, directly," David comments.

"Yes. It's a start of a whole new way of being for him. He'll probably get his fourth angel soon."

David moves to wipe away a tear.

"You don't cry," Angela scolds, albeit gently. "You're an angel."

David looks at his dry finger. "I wish I could cry. For joy."

Angela tilts her head as she hears something off in Emilyland. "Oh! She's waking up!"

The desert disappears...

...as Angela and David reappear with the other two angels in Emily's bedroom. A very sleepy Emily turns to look at the clock—11:58. She rolls onto her back, but she doesn't shut her eyes.

After studying the ceiling for a while, Emily looks over at the group of angels, specifically at David. He startles as her eyes seem to rest upon his, but it doesn't take long to realize that she's looking right through him. She holds out her hand to him; David starts to exclaim something to the others, but finds he's been awestruck into silence.

"Hold her hand," Angela urges him. After regaining his angelic composure, he complies.

Emily's mystified look turns to a smile as she realizes that, well, she might not be as alone in her room as she thought. She feels—well, something. She's not quite sure what, though. A scowl erases her smile as the practical, rational side of her mind takes over. She pulls her hand under her covers. For a very long time, David, whose hand remains up, where it was holding hers, remains more mystified than Emily was.

Brooke absentmindedly shuttles through the recordings of Jack's day: playing with his children, another less-than-exciting day at the office, playing with his children again, ignoring Lacey as much as humanly feasible, the gym. Day after day, the highlight is his children while the rest of the time seems to be a void of grey fog as Jack seems to just bumble through the actions of living with as little involvement as possible.

And how *is* that even possible? Brooke fiddles with some of the buttons along the top of the monitor. Much like her unknown counterpart, David, once toyed with "Dreamweaving," "Ultimate Wake Up," and "Special Programming Options" in the drop-down menu on the "Dream Implant" button, Brooke toys with the idea of pressing the on switch for a few of the items on the drop-down menu under "Life Lifting": "FutureFast,"

"Advanced Awakening," and "Align Human Being with Human Spirit." She lingers over that button for several seconds before another angelic hand comes to rest on hers.

She lets out a long sigh. "Wasn't going to."

"I know." Blake's complete understanding lifts her spirits a bit. "Want to go on a galactic gallivant?"

"A what?"

"On Earth they call it a 'road trip.' But our roads are a little bigger."

"We're allowed to do that?"

"Of course."

"Um, okay."

He takes her hand and they disappear from the desk...

...and Brooke finds herself standing just outside the Roman Coliseum. Two very jovial men dressed in gladiator costumes point the way to the entrance for a group of tourists. Brooke notices a few more men also in gladiator costumes, but their colors—both of their skin and of their costumes—are nowhere near as vibrant, and the men are nowhere near as cheery. Then she notices that there are a few more. And even a few more. As she and Blake pass through the walls to the inside arena, she sees many more humans who are certainly not gladiators—very tall women, very short men, people with physical handicaps, and others who would have been considered misfits in their time. And this time, still, perhaps, by the less-than-enlightened. Light beings in the shape of lions and other animals roam the grassy area that once was hidden under the grounds, the "playing" fields, of the coliseum.

"What?" Brooke blinks her eyes. Some of the dead fade as she makes her choice to see fewer of them. "Oh, of course. But why haven't they moved on yet?"

"Some have, some haven't."

Despite Brooke's attempts to fade the ghosts, she spies a woman way up in the highest seats. The woman would have been strikingly lovely were it not for the soul-deadening pain that fills her eyes. Brooke tunes in to the burning pain in her heart.

"Wow," she observes. "I guess sometimes the pain of not stopping something is greater than the pain of having it done to you."

"Yes, indeed," comes the response from her impressed superior.

Brooke scans the grounds again. The animals are definitely light beings, whereas most of the dead humans are not. Yet.

"They're still here to help the humans with their journeys," Blake clarifies. "Very few things in creation are as big as the love and devotion of an animal."

Brooke smiles at the idea and continues scanning. The walking dead shimmer a tad, but nowhere near as much as living humans do.

"What's going on with him?" Brooke points to one fellow who looks around, his eyes wide in horror, then covers his face with his hands as he cries.

"He's here now, he's still from the year 12 BCE, and he's also in the year 2782."

Brooke tries to wrap her angelic mind around that one.

"Don't worry about all that. They're on their journeys, too. For now, just see what's right here."

"Ummm...."

"Or not. Let's go somewhere else."

Blake starts to take her hand, but Brooke's attention is drawn to the words of a guide as he addresses a group finishing a tour: "Before you judge them for what they did, ask yourself what people two thousand years in the future will be judging you for—what you found entertaining or even acceptable in your society."

Brooke notices that even the people who died long ago have three angels. Blake notices her regarding an angel-with-a-laptop following one of the gladiators—one of the dead gladiators—in full calculating mode.

"Everything is just a thought," he tells her. "Everything. In this world, even in the worlds within worlds, even in the worlds within worlds within worlds, every cell of their bodies is a thought, every state of their affairs is a thought. And now there are seven billion humans on one planet. And what those angels are calculating are the highest chances for what is happening in this very moment, given all the things that could happen—change of heart, payment of a karmic debt, an infinite array of possibilities—what is most likely to happen for their human assignment. Even if that human no longer happens to be living in the physical world."

"Hmmmm." Brooke considers all the worlds within worlds within worlds as they are in living color—or not—right in front of her.

"Now, the thing about karma," Blake continues, "is there's really no such thing as karma. At least there's no karma from 'out there' determining how to even up a scoreboard. There's only what the human decides is his or her karma. Even Hitler has no karma—at least nothing from outside of him. He's created his own hell for himself, of course." He points to the angels with the lap-tops. "But every last bit of that is accounted for in their calculations so they can offer guidance."

"That the humans won't listen to."

"They do. Except when they don't. It's all good."

Blake lets Brooke ponder those words for several moments, and they disappear...

...and appear in a bathroom. A young man, the flesh of his bare chest and arms covered in tattoos, ears gauged, presses a razor blade to his wrist.

Brooke gasps. "I thought when you said 'Let's go somewhere else,' that meant it'd be a little easier."

"One place is always as good as another."

"Right. I believe you."

The young man's angels cry out to him. "Jason, you're needed here! This doesn't take care of anything! You can't skip steps. You want to make it here. You are so loved!"

At a knock on the door, Jason pushes the razor blade into his skin. His angels amplify their appeals to him. He stops. But with another knock, the razor goes slightly deeper. And, as his father kicks the door open, the cold metal pierces the vein and then—viciously, deeply—he slashes several other areas on the insides of both of his lower arms.

"Oh, Jason, no!" the man screams. "No, no, no, no!" He gathers his son into his arms. Jason's mother appears in the doorway, but not for long.

"Call 911," the father shrieks.

Brooke and Blake ride in the ambulance along with the young man, his parents, and an extremely active medical team who are applying bandages along with pressure to try to stem the bleeding.

"It's not time yet," Jason's head angel says to him.

"There's so much you came here to do," says another.

But losing the significant amount of blood—second to his desire—brings Jason's breathing and heart to a stop. This combination allows his light form to dislodge slightly from his physicality—hands and feet first, then his head, which is followed by the rest of his light body.

"He's not breathing," shouts one of the paramedics. Jason's parents sob.

"I don't want to stay," his spirit self tells his angels. "I don't. And I don't have to." He notices several light beings behind them. The light beings get brighter and brighter, especially one of them.

"Grandpa!" Jason's light self shouts.

"Everyone is welcomed home," Blake tells Brooke. "There are really no mistakes. They really can't get it wrong. And perhaps his leaving would be a necessary part of the paths of those around him. But...."

Jason's grandfather grabs him and holds him in a long, long embrace. Then he abruptly pushes him away.

"But Grandpa!"

His eyes shine and love streams from every inch of his entire being, but the grandfather shakes his head.

"I want to be with you," Jason beseeches. "I want to come home."

"Home is wherever you are," his grandfather says. "And however you are. Nothing of your soul's journey will change if you do this."

"But—"

"Not one thing would change. Yes, you can leave; you can do whatever you want. You can't get it wrong. But here, there, anywhere—your work has to be done. So you might as well stay and work it out. Make your home here on Earth and," he touches Jason's heart, "here."

Jason's hands and feet of light seem to dock, even click, back into his physical hands and feet. Then his head of light clicks into his physical head, followed by the rest of his light body clicking into his physical form.

The paramedic puts an ear to his mouth. "Wait, wait. He's still here. He's breathing," he smiles to the parents.

Jason's mother lets out a wail. "Thank you, thank you," she gushes between sobs. A defensive lineman might've had a hard time keeping her from pulling the medical team away. She drops to her knees beside the stretcher and wraps her arms around her son. Jason's father also kneels and wraps his arms around both of them.

Blake turns to Brooke. "So you see, there's really no way to get it wrong here," he says. "But some places may be better for them to be than others at any given point in time."

Brooke watches as the young man's parents continue to hold him and each other. Blake taps Brooke on her arm. "Alright, my lovely. It's time for some more field trips." He takes her hand in his and...

...Brooke finds herself in an emergency room in a hospital. Nurses and attendants rush a comatose woman, in her late twenties or so, by on a gurney. Her angels rush right alongside them and her.

"Didn't I just get this lesson?" she asks Blake. He glares at her, angelically. "Okay, okay," she whispers.

A doctor opens the woman's mouth to shove a tube down her throat.

"Eighteen pills," Blake tells Brooke. "Wow, she was serious."

"How do you know it was eighteen?"

Blake points to the woman's midsection. Brooke becomes aware of eighteen shadow pills passing through her upper stomach. Angels can count instantly, like some very mathematically advanced humans can.

A fifty-something woman rushes through the emergency waiting room, runs past the triage nurse despite her protest, dashes down the hall, and screams when she sees the young woman. "Brenda! Brenda! Oh, my baby, my baby!" She collapses onto her daughter. The nurses and attendants lift her off of Brenda.

Brooke notices a group of light beings gathering above Brenda, who looks up at them. Her light body starts to detach, hands and feet first. But the light beings shake their heads.

"Stay, Momma," a light being in the shape of a young girl, perhaps four in Earth years, says firmly. "It's not time to go yet."

"I miss you so much!" Brenda's light form cries to her.

"I'm right here, Momma," the young girl says. "I'm right by your side all the time. And it's fun over here. But it's not your time to go."

Brenda's light arms reach for her daughter as her own mother's arms reach for her. She holds her daughter at the same time the doctor allows her mother to hold her.

"I'm right here, always. And I'm fine." Her daughter slips from Brenda's embrace. "It's not your time yet!" she repeats.

Brenda's light form returns to her physical body, hands and feet docking and clicking in first, followed by her head and then the rest of her body.

One of her angels says to another, "We've been telling her that all night! Why'd she suddenly listen to her?"

Brooke notices that Brenda has four angels and that it was the trainee who had asked the question.

"If she was so high level—" she starts to ask Blake.

"Then why'd she do this?" Blake finishes for her. "All part of the journey. Maybe this was for someone else in her life."

As Brenda's spirit fully merges with her body, she starts coughing around the tube in her throat. Her mother screams.

"Probably her," Blake says, referring to the mother. "Looks like it was an important part of the learning on her journey, too."

Brooke nods. She notices that the room has been suffused with a rose-pink hue.

"And," Blake smiles, "there are even fewer things in creation bigger than the love and devotion of a human being, especially when that human being is a parent. On either side of the veil."

He takes Brooke by the hand and...

...Brooke finds herself standing in a garage. In full sway of the flow of creativity and passion, an artist flings paints here and there on a canvas the size of the wall. Music blares. He's almost dancing to his painting. Bewitched, Brooke watches a work of genius unfold.

The artist, a man in his late thirties, turns the music down, stands away from the canvas, and regards his work.

"I just want to paint!" he shouts to the canvas.

Brooke crosses her arms and brings one hand up to her face. "Um," she says to Blake through fingers drumming over her upper lip, "unless I'm mistaken, isn't that what he's doing?"

"Yes, that's exactly what he's doing. And that's exactly what he's calling for. But in his mind, he equates 'painting' with being a big-time artist, making lots of money, exhibiting in galleries all over the world, and, well, you get the picture."

"But he's not saying all that."

"No. And he's getting exactly what he's asking for. And it frustrates him no end because he could be as big as he wants to be. He's just, as the master teacher once said, 'Praying amiss.' He needs to be specific. The universe only picks up on 'painting' and his increasing frustration, and it responds with, 'Wow, he must really love being in that state because there he goes again.' The universe delivers whatever he's vibrating at."

Brooke nods, although her mind is whirling and swirling somewhat. "But doesn't the universe know what he means?"

"Life responds to clarity and intention. Muddled begets muddled." Blake claps his hands. "Alright, enough of a respite, back to some heavier-duty stuff."

"Ugh. This was pretty big. Really big. If only more people could understand this. This is really, really big." She's lollygagging—although this is indeed really, really big—as she has no desire to see heavier-duty stuff again. "Can't we go visit a frustrated sculptor or two?"

He takes her by the hand and they vanish from the garage...

...and Brooke finds herself standing on the Golden Gate Bridge. A woman calmly sits on a bench in the nearby park. Her angels beseech her to change her course of action. The woman's expression is stone. Brooke tries to hear her thoughts, but she finds that nothing is passing through the woman's mind.

"She's made it up," Blake says. "Her mind, that is."

"But obviously something's holding her back." The woman stands and heads toward the sidewalk leading to the bridge. "Okay, not anymore."

Her angels are beside themselves. "Janie, please! You've got to hear us! Janie, there's more for you!"

Brooke is beside herself wondering where the bridge officials, who are usually on a careful lookout for potential jumpers, are.

Janie holds the railing tightly, as if she's about to change her mind. She looks over at San Francisco—a luminous array of lights in the midst of the blackness of the water to the left and behind the city.

"It's so interesting that the jumpers here almost always jump on the side facing the city, with all the lights," Blake comments. "It's as if even in their darkest hour they still want the lights of their brothers and sisters to be with them."

Brooke looks over her shoulder to the black expanse off the west side of the bridge. Not very inviting— maybe especially so in someone's darkest hour.

"What people don't realize is that there's really nowhere to go. They'll still be just as alive on the other side."

"Will they have some kind of punishment waiting for them?"

"Whatever they decide," Blake says. "Every soul gets to write its own story."

The woman continues walking. Her mind is still quiet, resolute, at peace. No longer pleading with her, the angels surrounding her start speaking along a very different track: "We love you, Janie. You are love. Go with love. We'll see you on the other side. We love you. Love is all there is."

"Will they have a harder job next time?"

"What makes you ask that?"

"Because, well," Brooke hesitates, "this one wasn't exactly a success."

The woman jumps. After what seems to Brooke like an interminable passage of time, she hears a splash. If she could, she'd weep.

Blake puts his arm around her. "There's never a failure," he whispers. "Ever. Just evolution. And then, more evolving. And then, more evolving. That's what creation does."

"But won't she have to pay for that at some point?"

"They advance not because of karma or something outside of themselves judging them or dictating to them. They evolve because it's the thing to do. That's what creation does," Blake repeats. He pauses for a moment. "Always and forever and everywhere."

"So everyone gets to go home?"

"No."

Brooke looks at him, puzzled.

"You heard Jason's grandfather. Everyone's already home." At Brooke's bewilderment, he adds, "Doesn't mean home couldn't use a remodeling. New drapes, new furniture, new perspective—especially the new perspective. Drapes won't cut it without that. Humans always, always have that choice. Always. And forever. And everywhere."

CHAPTER 5

SLAM! The cell door closes behind Jack.

Okay, maybe we shouldn't have sprung that on you quite so suddenly. If we all back up a little, we would see Jack, après gym, being pulled over by a policeman because his car's left taillight was out. The cop was a little bored that night, and Jack seemed inordinately deadpan, almost zombie-like, so he asked Jack to step out of the car while he checked it. The only person more astounded to discover drugs in the trunk was Jack.

So if we back up a little more, we would see Dick putting the drugs in the trunk as well as monkeying with the taillight. And if we back up even more, we would see Jack's angel team working for four—four!— years to help him wake up. Nothing! Finally, the Big Boss intervened in a Big Way.

And a few weeks before we would've seen Dick putting the drugs in the car, we would've seen a very interesting scene in Jack's living room. One night, for some reason, Lacey stuck by Jack's side as he read to the children and tucked them in. None of them wanted her intruding on the special father-child time, but she was oblivious to the strong emotions that were trying to push her out of the room. After the reading time, she held Chelsea and then, later, Ben. "Let's say a prayer.

Let's ask Jesus to keep you safe and make everything all right for you tonight, tomorrow, and always."

Chelsea and Ben complied, but they weren't happy about it. Not because they had anything against Jesus, but because, well, they had something against their mother, even if she was their mother. Oh sure, they loved her, but that didn't mean they wanted her around at bedtime, normally their favorite time of day.

When Jack and Lacey left the sleeping children and drifted into the living room, Jack turned to her. "We need to talk."

"About what?"

"Jesus!" It came out much stronger than Jack had intended.

"Jack, don't swear at me. Just tell me what you want to talk about."

"Jesus!" He was so upset that he couldn't say the hundreds, perhaps thousands of additional words that were flooding his brain.

"Jack, stop swearing at me! What do you want to talk about?"

"Christ!"

Lacey stormed out of the room. Jack had been finding himself, much to his own surprise, reading, searching, researching, and reading some more. If Jack's sudden upset hadn't tied up his tongue, he might've said something along the lines of, "Jesus was a master teacher, one of the most important teachers humanity has ever had. He wasn't telling people to believe in *him*, but to believe in what he was teaching. He doesn't want people to rely on *him* to keep them safe, rather to rely on their own inner power, which is what he was trying to teach them about."

But, as you now know, it didn't come out exactly like that. Not even remotely like that. Lacey flipped. She suddenly realized that the main thing, other than the children, that had been keeping her with Jack—their shared religion—looked like it was fading away. So she did what any upstanding, moral person would do. She consulted with her boyfriend.

And that leads us back to Dick putting the drugs in the car. Oh, you might think setting up false charges happens rarely. It actually happens fairly often. And you might think that prison is an unnecessarily hard and unjust challenge to face. But then so is getting tortured, raped, murdered. So is having a parent die when you're a child or having a child die when you're a parent. Or having a loved one disappear without a trace. Or losing loved ones and all worldly possessions in a flood, earthquake, mudslide, or forest fire. Or in a war—and most absurd of all is a war in the name of God. This might have worked back when Earthlings were trying to explain where lightning bolts came from, and having a god of war seemed as likely as a god of weather, but it's way passé at this point in existence.

All of these seemingly random things seem so...well, random. But every being in eternity has...well, eternity. We never know what challenges a being has called into his or her life to experience in order to grow, learn, evolve. Our discussion of this isn't meant to minimize the pain endured in tragedies. And it's not to blame the victim. Indeed, it's to empower every human being. There actually are no pawns, no victims. But there must be responsibility, and in that comes personal power. There are no kings, no victors, either. It's all...... Life.

And you want to know what's really strange? Humans sometimes want to be like the other beings in the universe. But do you know how many beings are lined up waiting to be human? They know where it's at.

And you humans can't mess it up. Even Jack, even Dick, even anyone. Winning awaits everyone at the end of a long day, or a long lifetime as the case may be. Or, better yet, winning awaits everyone in every moment—awareness of that fact is the only requirement.

While we're talking about it all, which we guess we always are, here and everywhere, you might think Lacey and Dick are being, well, bad. Villains. But there are no villains; there's just another side of a story, another sovereign being playing out his or her part on the grand stage with other sovereign beings. The rapist has been raped in his (or even her) life and plays that out. The warlord has been ravaged and seeks to play that out. Or he will be ravaged. Or the rapist will be raped, one way or another. Everyone has his or her part to play. Everything anyone does can be understood from the higher point of view.

Or, as in Dick's case, it also just might be possible that he or she just signed up to be a real Class-A jerk in this lifetime!

Back to our story. A few days prior to the cell door slamming, the angel team was still batting ideas around until Blake went for a private conference with the Big Boss. He even stayed in conference when Jack woke up, leaving the other three to attend to Jack without him—an extremely unusual thing for a head angel to do. It's nearly unheard of, except in extreme circumstances. Brooke noticed that Jack was especially out of it that day, almost like he was sleepwalking. Technically, he was. But much more about that much later.

Later that night, when Jack was circumnavigating the universe—oh, sorry, we mean sleeping—Blake returned to the group. "So, well, um, hmmmmm. Prison is always a good place for waking up."

The laptop and the microphone and the mouse were dropped, as were three angelic jaws.

"Say what?"

"Prison?"

"But he's such a good guy. He even obeys the speed limits."

"Well, we'll just have to find something," Blake responds. "We can make something up if we have to. And I guess we'll have to. Wasn't my idea."

The group is silent for a moment as it considers why in creation.....

"Okay, how?"

"Okay, what?"

"There's nothing on this guy. He's as straight-laced as they come."

"Hmmm, we'll need some human intervention for this one. How about Dick, his boss? He's a greedy, tenacious SOB. I mean, he's a beautiful being of the divine, cleverly disguised as a greedy, tenacious SOB. And he wants Lacey. Well, he can have her. So let's have him do something."

"And then what will happen to Dick?" Brooke asks.

"The right reward for greedy SOBs. Business disaster, divorce, kids will hate him, a plague or two."

"Which one?"

"Yes."

"All of 'em?"

"All of 'em."

"Yes," Christopher says, consulting the computer he retrieved from the floor. "He's the one to do it. He's friends with a judge and a U.S. attorney and a drug dealer."

"What about Jack's poor children?" Brooke moans. "They'll be without their father. For years, perhaps."

Christopher punches some other codes into the laptop. "Let's see, what did they sign up for in this lifetime? Hmmmmmmmmmm. Ah, here it is. Forgiveness, compassion, overcoming adversity. Well, this would certainly fall into teaching them those lessons."

"And what did Dick sign up for?"

Christopher punches a few other codes into the computer. "Hmmmm, okay, great, he signed up to assist someone's growth in any way he could. He would certainly be doing this for Jack's highest good."

"But what about his punishments?" Brooke asks. "How could life punish someone who's actually doing someone a favor?"

Blake puts his hand on her shoulder, as she's frenzied herself into quite the swivet. "The helpers know going in that they'll suffer for being despicable. That's all part of the lesson they choose, all part of the game."

"Great game," Brooke murmurs.

"Would you design it any differently?"

After recovering from her surprise at the question, Brooke takes a few minutes to deeply ponder potential possibilities. "No. I wouldn't."

"It's really ingenious, isn't it?"

More pondering. "Yes. It is."

A flabbergasted Jack stands before a very stern judge in a courtroom.

"Your sentence will be no less than three years." The judge's gavel crashes onto the bench.

Jack's lawyer is as stunned as his client. "This is absolutely lunacy," he calls to Jack as he is lead out of the courtroom by the bailiff. "This was a trumped-up, bogus charge. We'll have another judge for your appeal and get you out."

The family of four tries to visit in a packed room that is more like a bus station than a visiting room. Ben and Chelsea sit on either side of Jack, and he wraps an arm around each. Lacey, sitting on the other side of Chelsea, grunts.

A baby screams in the background, making it very difficult for Jack's soft voice to be heard. "As soon as I'm out on appeal," he says to Lacey, "we'll start living the life we always dreamed about."

Christopher drops his computer, Sapphire stops whispering, and Brooke and Blake hang their mouths wide open. The angel team surrounds him, waving their fists in the air, wanting to strangle him. Angelically.

Over a year later, a big, red DENIED stamp slams down onto Jack's appeal papers.

Jack lies on his bunk, blankly staring into space and shaking his head ever so slightly in disbelief. He releases a very, very long sigh. He unclenches his fists, opens his hands, and rests them on the bed, palms up.

Emily walks into her mother's nursing home room, sits on the bed, and takes her mother's hand. "Mom," she whispers.

"My Emily. It won't be long now."

"Oh, Mom, now don't talk like that."

Okay, perhaps we shouldn't have sprung that one on you quite so suddenly either. While Jack's angels were working with him for all those years, Emily's angels were working with her, too—and then for even one more year. Her angels, except for David, also met with the Big Boss many times during that period, but nothing as flamboyant as prison was determined for her.

In that time, Barbara decided she was done with the Earth phase of her journey. At least, her soul made that decision and, as a result, her body became inordinately tired as some cells became inordinately active, even more than they did years back, before the disease went into remission.

Just for the record, sometimes beings come in with a certain timeline, sometimes not. Depends. The future is always...well, you could recite the answer by now.

"I will talk like that, thank you very much. I don't have much talking left to do, and I want to make every word count as much as possible."

Emily starts to protest, but the reality of her mother's words hits her heart with a sharp pang. Barbara smiles at her, and she tries to smile in return. Out of habit, both as a flower maven and a compulsive taskdoer, she starts to get some more water for the flowers. But she stops and slowly sits back down, realizing that no task could be more important than any words at this point. "Are you scared, Mom?"

"Heavens, no. Will you be, when you go?"

"I doubt it." Emily studies the family photographs, sitting next to a special heirloom vase filled with roses, all of which Barbara had requested for her bedside table. "Do you think about Dad?"

"All the time. You know I never wanted to get married again because I already had the best husband in the world."

"As you've told me only a million times."

"There was no topping him. No way, no how."

"You've told me that a million times, too. Maybe a billion."

"And just think—now I get to be with him again. Oh, I can't wait!"

Emily studies another picture on the table. "You'll get to see Lisa."

"Yes." After some fumbling to free her hands of her bedcovers and despite her weakness, her mother reaches out to take both of her daughter's hands. "Emily, I want you to be happy. When are you going to let that happen?"

"Soon."

"Promise?"

"Yes."

"I believe you."

"I will!"

"Promise?"

"Yes! Otherwise, you'll still be bugging me from the other side about it."

Sunshine pours through the window, casting the room in a warm, golden glow. Barbara releases Emily's hands, and Emily finds sudden fascination with tracing a finger along the petals of a wide-open rose, relishing their softness.

"You can bet on that. But that's not the reason to let yourself be happy. It's not some bourgeois activity, you know, this happiness thing. It's what you're here for."

Emily continues her tracing.

"I'm surprised Lisa isn't bugging you more about it."

"Maybe she is. Still in the way a ten-year-old would."

"You didn't have to leave life with her, my sweet Emily. Can you let yourself live at last?"

Ching!

"Just at the nursing home?" Marion gently asks.

Emily nods. As always, the heavy scent of flowers and soil calms her.

"How's she doing?"

Emily shrugs, then slowly shakes her head.

"She's had such a full and rich life," Marion smiles. "All used up—and very well used—and no regrets. That's the way to go."

Emily nods. She is surprised at the peace she feels amidst the sorrow, and it was from a place far deeper than the scent of flowers and soil.

Sam climbs into bed and tries to gauge if Emily's asleep or if she's just pretending. (He knows, of course—no one can be that out of it. And Emily knew that he knew, and he knew that Emily knew that he knew, and she knew that he knew that, too.) He taps Emily on the shoulder.

"NO!"

Ching! Once again, the door broadcasts Emily's arrival at the flower shop/healing locus. Once again, another morning's fight with Sam has left her beyond frazzled.

"Good morning." Once again, Marion smiles as she greets Emily while tending to an ornate flower arrangement. "How are you, dear one?"

Once again, Emily bursts into tears, which quickly wend their way to wailing. And, once again, while Emily's angels cover their ears, Marion calmly retrieves the box of tissues for her.

When the wails subside, David slaps his hand on his thigh, angelically. "How can she be so at peace that her mother, her best friend, is dying, but then be such a wreck over...."

"Nothing?" Angela snipes.

"They're very good at the big things. Maybe because they galactisize the smaller things."

Angela slaps her hand on her thigh, angelically, but for a different reason than David. Her cackles resound through the shop.

After a quick glance around her store, as if hearing something very strange, Marion enfolds Emily in a hug. "You have eternity, dear one. But you might want to get started on the happy part of eternity sooner than later."

"Hey, she's still taking our job!" David laughs.

Jack's lawyer places a stack of papers on the visiting-room table. "Your wife is suing you for a divorce."

The feelings flooding through Jack's entire body amaze him. That night, staring up from his bunk bed, he is still amazed. "You know," he announces to the ceiling, "I felt more imprisoned with her than I feel in here."

From the depths under his top bunk comes the voice of Raymond, his bunkie. "Man, I didn't want to tell you this, but you never sounded like you thought much of her, respected her, even liked her."

"Ever hear that saying, be careful what you ask for?" Jack asks, the question more for himself than his friend. "I asked for more time to read and meditate. I asked for more time to work out. I asked for time to get a master's degree. I asked for her to file for divorce, because she would make life hell for me if I pursued it first." Jack sits up. "And it all happened. But it happened by default. I'm done living that way. I'm going to figure out exactly what I want for the rest of my life, and how I want to live it, and who I want to live it with."

He pulls out a notebook and starts to write.

Dawn arrives and finds Jack still staring at the ceiling as he lies in his bunk. He pulls out his journal, writes a few more notes, and then lies back down again. After a moment of trying to sleep, he sits up and meditates. His angels meditate with him.

By the way, ever wish you could see what the angels see and do what the angels do? You can, and do.

The leaves on the tree just outside the window, via their caress by the gentle wind, create a dance of sunlight on the kitchen floor. The cats pounce on the moving spots, lifting Emily out of her slump for a moment. The moment is short-lived, however, as Sam coughs, yanking her back from the dancing sunspots and into her self-inflicted misery. Oh, sure, she knows it's self-inflicted. And she's getting tired of it. She suddenly imagines that life is an ongoing etching and sketching plaything. Don't like the picture? Shake it up and draw a new one. Don't like that picture? Shake and draw again. And again.

Emily rises from the breakfast table and relishes the loud clatter as she drops her dishes into the sink. A very startled Sam lowers the paper just long enough to shoot her a withering glance. But Emily doesn't much feel like being withered today. She walks outside, leaving the room and its objectionable ambiance behind her.

She picks a couple of cherry tomatoes off the potted vine just outside the kitchen door. She pops them in her mouth, one after the other, tasting the warmth of the morning sun and the cleansing of yesterday's rain in their tart sweetness.

Her cats follow her as she ambles along the path to the driveway. She picks them up and holds them close to her. The clouds play with the sunshine on the mountains, a much grander version of the light show on her kitchen floor.

The next thing Emily knows is that she is much closer to those clouds as she sits in her car halfway up the very tall mountain close to her town. The clock showed that more than an hour had passed, but she has no awareness of the time passing nor how she got there.

David would tell you, "That'd be us!"

Emily climbs out of her car, soaking in the scenery, the fresh air, the sunshine on her face. It strikes her as strange how few cars are in the parking lot, given this day just made for hiking. She pulls a blanket out of the trunk and starts along the trail.

Several minutes later, a grassy spot on the hillside beckons to her to abandon the path. She spreads out her blanket and then spreads out her long body and limbs on top of it. She gazes at the sky and the tops of the pine trees in a nearby grove. She could swear the trees are whispering to her.

Laughter from the trail causes her to look back in that direction. A mother and father, who are about Emily's age, with their daughter, about ten years old, seem to find their hike very amusing. But their amusement is a sharp contrast to the sudden, searing pain in her heart. A mother, a father, a ten-year-old girl. She is losing her mother, has lost her father, has not only lost her twin sister when they were both ten, but also at this point in her life would probably never have a ten-year-old or a child of any age. She and Sam had tried, but she was never very disappointed that their attempts had failed—until this very minute.

Her tears and sobs come so fast, so furious, so hot, so deep that she struggles to breathe. She cannot see or hear her angels consoling her, but even through the keening that seems to be emitting from her entire body, not just from her heart and throat, she feels the ground under her. It's almost as if Earth is cradling her, drawing her pain out of her. If she could see her angels, she would see David holding her hand.

What does come to her sight is a light beam originating from the center of the planet up through her body and up to the farthest ethers. And even way, way beyond that.

Note to you, our reader: that's how big you are. No, big-ger. No, bigger than that, even. Yes, really. And when you get into fear of any kind, you shrink. No, smaller. No, smaller than that, even. Yes, really.

In this minute, Emily gets that. Really. She lies in her blissful, expanded state for a long, long while. A gentle breeze stirs her, and she opens her eyes. The low rays of the sun alert her that night would soon be coming, so she prepares to go home.

Home. Her beautiful home that she loves so much. But just the thought of seeing Sam bursts the bigness, the bubble of infinity she'd been reveling in for hours and hours. Poof! Back to small.

That night, David watches Emily's sleep-and-dream monitor:

On a beach, two children run into her arms and the three tumble to the sand. The laughing puddle of three becomes a pond of four as a man joins the laughfest.

The dream stops abruptly as Emily tosses and turns in her bed. Once assured that he won't need to be popping into her room at any second, David turns to watch her day-in-review.

Bliss shines on Emily's face as she weeds the garden and then picks a few vegetables.

"The universe has already given them everything," he sighs to Angela. "All of them. Everything. It might not be in the form of millions of dollars, the new house, the new car, the ten-year-old child, but the universe is a place where all is provided. One way or another. Part of the game is drawing that—literally—into their lives. They can draw the picture."

"Think you could do better?"

"I sure hope I would!"

"What's the thing you'd try to remember if you ever did the human gig?"

"Shake and draw. Shake and draw. Like that toy Emily was thinking about."

"Anything else?"

"Remember this conversation."

"Good luck with that! All humans go to Earth thinking they'll remember all the conversations like this one. But so few do. That's part of the point."

"Great."

Brooke watches the monitor that shows the overview of Jack's day:

As he washes dishes in the prison kitchen, the thermometer on the wall behind him reads one hundred and twenty degrees.

In the prison's weight room, with the help of a couple of other inmates, a getting-very-buff-and-handsome Jack lifts a set of heavy weights over his head.

Just down the hall from the television room, Jack lounges on a sofa with a book. He sits up, pulls out his notebook, and writes a few words.

That night, Jack lies down in his bunk and falls asleep instantly.

Well, it was almost instantly. There was enough time for him to say something to whomever was listening: "Thank you."

Very strange how things work out sometimes, isn't it?

Jack walks the track en route to the bleachers, a book tucked under his arm. His shoulders are no longer hunched, plus he's not really walking—he's strolling. Cool. Strolling cool was far from his repertoire B.P. as he refers to it (Before Prison, but you probably figured that one out). Several inmates walking the track toward him nod their heads politely and step out of his way.

"Morning, Mr. Anderson," one calls to him.

"Name's Jack," he calls back.

"Yes, Mr. Anderson."

Another inmate approaches and walks along the track with him. "Good morning, Mr. Anderson."

"Name's Jack."

"I'd love to talk to you about something, Mr. Anderson. Have you been saved?"

Jack thinks for a moment about how he wants to respond. "As a matter of fact, I have been."

"So you know you're going to Heaven?"

No thinking is required this time. "I'm already in Heaven."

He gives an understanding smile to his fellow inmate's obvious confusion. He takes a seat on the bleachers and opens his book.

That night, Brooke again watches the review of Jack's day:

The inmate who asked Jack if he was saved sits by him on the bleachers and they talk.

Jack and the same inmate talk while they push their lunch trays through the cafeteria line. They sit down at a table together, still talking.

Jack wanders into the prison's music/game room where he picks up a guitar and starts to play. Another inmate joins him and shows him how to play a few chords.

Amidst the usual din of the inmates calling to and joking with each other before lights out, Jack meditates on his bunk.

With snores echoing down the hall, Jack stares at the darkened ceiling. A smile spreads across his face.

Shifting her view to the other monitor, Brooke watches Jack sleep. As Christopher and Sapphire attend to their tasks, Blake touches Brooke's arm. "Something's on your mind."

Brooke sighs. "It's the strangest thing about humans—if you put them in a bad situation, they rise. If you put them in a good situation, they sink. Not always, of course, but sometimes."

"Well, there can always be something good about the bad and something not so good about the good."

"He's become gallant. Confident. So much more than he was."

"I hear a 'but' in there."

"But did it have to happen this way? And what about Dick, the guy who got him sent to prison? What happened to him? I know you said awful things were going to befall him, but didn't he sign up to help someone awaken?"

"Yes, he did. But if he chooses not to awaken, the guilt will make him sick."

"Will his angels arrange all that?"

"Well, not really. His angels don't really have to do anything in that regard. When people are unkind, unhappy, disgruntled, their bodies fill with toxins that can make them sick, prematurely age them, and cause them to die a miserable death."

Brooke digests this information.

"Or not. Depends."

"Oh, thanks!"

"Take smiling, for instance. When someone is genuinely happy, why even the mere act of moving the facial muscles into a smile does a world of good for his or her body. Meditating and smiling and being kind and good-hearted does a lot more good than a good heart doctor or a good plastic surgeon. And laughing massages the internal organs. Living a life of peace and joy and being true to the self keeps the cardiologist away."

Brooke digests this information, too.

"Or not. Depends."

"Oh, thanks again!"

"Everything always depends on other thoughts, actions, effects, choices, decisions made before incarnating, the highest path for the soul's evolution, and the same items coming from seven billion other human beings." He stops as Brooke starts to swoon from information overload. "But true happiness can be the ultimate elixir."

"But Dick signed up to do something good, really."

"Well, yes, but he's forgotten his mission—almost all of them do when they come here—and he's gotten lost in his character. He's become a greedy, self-centered, narrow-minded man. What comes to him is the direct effect of that cause. It can change in an instant. The whole future can change in an instant of awakening. He could make amends, he could forgive himself, and he could awaken to the whole shadow play, the whole scenario."

Brooke adjusts the dial on a monitor and watches Dick sleeping peacefully. "But he seems like he's doing just fine."

"He's not very advanced. It'll all take a while to catch up with him. Now if Jack did something like this, he'd have instant karma, delivered by himself. The more advanced the being, the faster the repercussions come when he or she fumbles the ball."

"It's all very complicated."

"Don't make yourself crazy. The bottom line is life is good. And humans can catch on in infinite ways. Just might take them a while to get there."

"Hmmmmm."

"For Jack's own path, it's not up to Dick to apologize; it's up to Jack to get over it. And he did."

"Hmmmmm."

"You can't flunk Earth. You can't lose this ball game. You get to go back over and over 'til you get it right."

"You keep saying you! Not me!"

"No, no, I mean humans, of course."

CHAPTER 6

Brooke and Blake study a snapshot of a page from Jack's journal on a monitor while the sleeping-and-dreaming Jack is shown on the upper-left monitor. Delightful dream blips pop and fade around his head, mostly involving a tall, beautiful, joy-filled woman:

She disappears into a forest, then reappears on a beach. She disappears into the ocean amidst a pod of dolphins, then reappears on a tiny island, but then she dives into the waves. She passes by him in her car, then disappears down the freeway. She dashes across a sun-dappled meadow, then disappears into the shadows at the far edge of the field. He calls to her and is overjoyed to see her reappear from the shadows.

"Alright," Blake says to his protégé. "He's clearly convinced he's going to meet her any moment after his release. You take on this part of this ball game. Go ahead, hit it right on out of the ballpark."

"So," Brooke announces to the rest of the group, "he's getting out of prison soon and he wants a wife. Not just any wife—he has a list of forty things there."

"Forty!" Sapphire frowns. "No one ever makes a list of forty qualities in a mate. That'd be impossible."

"Nothing's impossible," Blake reminds her.

"Possible for us, maybe," Sapphire groans. "We're angels." She points to the sleeping Jack as bits of his dreams continue to show up on the monitor. "This one's another story."

"The qualities on the list are about one-third physical, one-third emotional and intellectual, and one-third spiritual," Brooke continues. "And he's crystal, crystal clear about it all. Plus, he's willing to wait for the whole enchilada, even until the next lifetime if he has to. But his work and healing show he's ready for her now. So now the question is, how are we going to find someone who fits all those things?"

Christopher reads each quality on the list aloud and types it into his computer. "Long hair. Beautiful. Intelligent. At peace with her world. Conscious. Has done her work. Not too fussy, is he?" Christopher starts to enter the next requisite attribute but stops. "Six feet tall. Is he over six feet tall? I guess he is, now that he's standing up straight." He finishes entering the information on his laptop and presses the return key.

As the new information appears on the screen, Blake studies it carefully. "Well," he says, "it looks like there's a woman in Idaho who matches every one of these things. Only one problem."

"What's that?" Brooke asks.

"She's married."

"Married! That's obviously not going to work." Brooke pauses for a moment. "Well, how married?"

Blake studies the screen. "Hmmmm, a tiny, tiny spark of love is still there, but the two are no longer a suitable team. They're not on each other's ballpark, I mean wavelength, and not interested in the same game anymore. At all."

"Where are her angels?" Brooke asks. "Let's talk to them."

Christopher punches more information into the computer. Blake reads the results and then stands up, looking over his shoulder. "They're right over there."

Brooke follows the direction his finger is pointing. "Right over there" in such an enormous hall in this case equals about two football fields in Earth terms. When Brooke finally sees the cubicle he's pointing out, she finds herself looking at an empty desk.

"She must be a night owl, too."

At the sound of footsteps on the stairs, Emily turns away from the door and pretends to be asleep. Sam crawls into bed and, after a moment, taps her on the shoulder. Emily ignores him and continues to pretend she's asleep. At this point, since both of them know, it's not really pretending; it's out-and-out dissing.

A few moments later, Emily hears a snore. Sam's angels disappear to the great office in the sky. Emily looks at the clock: 12:12. She rolls onto her back and stares at the ceiling.

Emily looks at the clock again: 2:22. She continues her concentrated study of the ceiling, made possible by a waning gibbous moon shining through the bedroom window. Stephanie computes, Jasper whispers, and Angela watches David pace.

"Emily," David pleads, "you have to—" He turns to Angela. "Oh, I've said it all ten thousand times before. I'm not even exaggerating about the number."

"I know you're not, but say it again," Angela says. "Time number ten thousand and one might be the time that she hears it."

David stands over Emily, positioning his head between her and the ceiling. Her eyes would be looking at his if she could see him. "You," he says to her, "are here to do really great things. You do them sometimes—in your dreams. It's not like you have to win the Nobel Peace Prize or anything like that, but you could devote your life to your own version of greatness, the greatest you there could be."

A tear rolls down Emily's cheek. David could swear she saw him, for just an instant; he and Angela exchange glances. Emily holds out her hand to the semi-darkness—that's only the second time she's done that, and it's the first in many years. David takes her hand and lowers his cheek to it. Emily smiles through her tears. David tries to catch a tear as it slips down her face, but of course it passes through his finger. When he examines his finger, though, he could swear it was ever so slightly damp.

At Jack's angel team's desk, while Sapphire whispers and Christopher computes, Brooke and Blake pace, occasionally looking over at Emily's angels' still-empty desk. Angels have exceptionally keen eyesight, as you can probably well imagine, so seeing something the distance of two football fields away is not a challenge.

"What does she do," Brooke wonders aloud, "night-time security guard?"

"Lady of the evening?" Blake suggests.

"Oh, that would be great for an ex-con." She pauses, but speaks before Blake has a chance to. "I know, it's all divine."

Christopher looks up the information. "She works in a flower shop."

"That wasn't a nighttime occupation, last I knew."

The clock now reads 3:33. David, Angela, Jasper, and Stephanie huddle around Emily, who has returned to her study of the ceiling, all the brighter with the moon lower in the sky and more fully shining in her window.

"Emily, there's more for you to do," David says.

"Emily, you can give so much more," Angela joins in. "It would bring you so much more happiness. If this is your definition of happiness, you need to expand your dictionary to the cosmic edition."

"But," David says, "perhaps for right now a good night's sleep would help get you going."

Emily rolls over and shuts her eyes. Her four angels smile as they look at each other. Did she hear those words? After a moment, they disappear...

...and appear at their desk.

"Whew, thought she'd never fall asleep tonight," David says to no one in particular.

To their great surprise, Emily's four angels notice an angel team staring at them from across an expanse of two hundred yards. There's something about a deliberate stare—it's felt, no matter how far away it is.

"Was it something we said?" David asks Jack's team.

Angels also have exceptionally keen hearing, as you can also probably well imagine, especially for whatever is meant for them to hear. Even intergalactically, let alone in the big hall.

"We have to talk to you," Brooke says. She and the rest of her group transport themselves over and converge on Emily's angels' desk.

Emily's four angels cluster around her as she folds laundry in her bedroom. While Stephanie and Jasper attend to their tasks, David and Angela walk in circles around their human.

"I told you," Angela tells him, "this is your special project. So get going."

"Emily," David says, "we've found the perfect man for you. The problem is, you're still married, but on paper only, not in your heart. You'll need to change that."

"Life," Emily says to the air, "if you want me to leave him, you're going to have to take him from me—in a good way, thank you, don't kill him or anything like that—because I'm not leaving him. I made a promise. I don't like to give up on things." Emily stops her folding in mid-motion and looks around her. "Where in the world did that come from?" she asks her cats. They lovingly oblige her with no response except slow blinks of their huge eyes. Emily returns to her chore.

After recovering from their shock, her four angels hoot, holler, and give each other high fives and fist bumps. Highly annoyed, the cats slip out of the room—too much commotion for their old cat selves.

"She's getting it!" David shouts.

Sam appears in the doorway. "Emily, I think it's time we go our separate ways."

The only one of Emily and her four angels who doesn't do a double take is Emily. Her angels look at Sam's angels for an explanation; they shrug.

"Beats us," the angelic version of the fat slob says. "Just happened."

"Well, that was quick!" David says. "Way to manifest, Emily!"

"Okay." Emily continues her folding.

More than just a little surprised at her nonchalance, Sam leaves. Emily sits on the bed, lets out a long sigh, smiles, thinks for a moment, and—out comes the wail.

"At least she doesn't keep it all bottled up inside," David says.

"Perish the thought," says Angela.

Jack and Emily's angels crowd around double the amount of computer screens, which they've moved to be side by side on a larger desk in a larger cubicle. Jack's day-in-review plays on a monitor:

In street clothes, Jack shakes hands with numerous inmates and then several prison officials, even the office secretary.

As he leaves the gate, he spots Ben and Chelsea racing across the sidewalk. Jack bends down and his children fall into his arms while Irene stands by her car at the curb. The angels concur that picking up an ex-son-in-law from prison is a class act for an ex-mother-in-law.

Irene opens the door of an apartment and leads Jack and the children inside. The elegant-but-still-appropriate-for-a-single-dad living room has a large window facing the ocean. She shows Jack, Ben, and Chelsea their bedrooms one by one, although the family tour is a cumbersome affair as the three stay stuck together like glue, needing to maneuver slowly through halls and doorways.

Jack's room has a king-size bed and well-appointed sitting area in front of a large window also facing the ocean. The theme for Ben's room is Modern American Little League—on the bedspread, the curtains, even on the walls. Chelsea has a fairy-princess motif, complete with a canopy of pink lace billowing out from a decorative light in the center of the ceiling, plus an enchanted forest on the wall painted by Jack's former coworker from years ago.

Irene opens the refrigerator and cabinet doors to reveal a fully stocked kitchen. As she leaves, she hands Jack a check for ten thousand dollars. He tries to give it back to her, but she refuses it. (By this time, you've probably sensed that she knew about Lacey all along, of course; Jack would never request any assistance from her, but she wanted to help him, and she had to wait until his release before she could do anything for him and keep it private.)

Jack, Ben, and Chelsea clutch each other as the Ferris wheel at the Santa Monica Pier reaches its apex. The children point to the setting sun over the Pacific. Jack's expression reveals that he wants for absolutely nothing in this moment.

Jack sits first with Chelsea and then with Ben at bedtime.

There was no reading this night; the children just wanted to talk to their father, alone, for the first time in three years. That was a year shy of being a third of Ben's life and a year shy of being half of Chelsea's life. But what they end up creating out of this experience are their own books in the future. Right now, back to the task facing the two angel teams.

"They could meet online," Blake suggests.

"Too cliché," Angela says.

"How about an airplane?" David offers.

Brooke pretends to snore.

"How about a car accident?" Jasper asks. "I mean, not a bad car accident—just bad enough to get them out of their cars so they can bump into each other."

"Hmmmmm," say seven other angels in unison.

"There might be something to that," says Angela.

"That might be a good play." You know that was Blake.

Stephanie types in some information.

Blake reads the screen. "Hey, look, a huge traffic accident is supposed to happen in three weeks in L.A. right near the Staples Center the afternoon before a big concert. Lots of reasons why—thousands of 'em, really. Is there any way we can get her there in time?"

"Oh, but of course there is," Sapphire says, a slight edge of peevishness in her voice. "We're angels."

David and Brooke whirl around to face her direction, their utter astonishment utterly apparent, but she ignores them both. After they slowly turn back to the computer monitors, she glares at their backs.

Blake nudges her. "Just keep the focus on your position in the game."

Grabbing her microphone, Sapphire returns to her whispering, peevishness notwithstanding. "What? I'm whispering, I'm whispering," she hisses to mollify the incredulous expression on Jasper's face.

"Some divine discontent brewing," Blake explains to Angela.

"One of the most powerful forces in the world," Angela replies.

David fiddles with some dials for a moment. "I don't think Emily has to be actually in an accident. I don't want her waylaid any more than she already has been."

"Well, she doesn't have to have a bad accident," Angela says. "Like Jasper said, maybe she could just be nearby one big enough to get her attention."

"That'll have to be huge," David says.

"How are we going to get Jack there?" Brooke asks. "He's never in that part of town at that time of day."

"Well at least he lives somewhat near there now," David says. "Closer than he was before, anyway."

"We can make sure he gets a job near there, too," Blake says. "Or at least one that will send him over to that area then."

"On it." Christopher starts inputting data.

"But how in creation are we going to get Emily to L.A.?" David asks.

"One of the primary reasons she's been staying in Idaho is for her mother. She won't need to do that much longer."

The other seven angels pause as they realize what Angela has just stated. Stephanie switches the dial under one of the monitors to reveal Barbara asleep in a hospital bed. Light radiates from her while numerous light beings hover nearby.

"No, not long," Christopher says.

The eight of them look at the monitor revealing a sound-asleep Emily, a somewhat blissful expression lighting up her face. Jack's monitor shows that he has entered deep sleep, and a blissful expression beams on his face, as well.

Stephanie returns to studying the information on her laptop. "There's an art-and-flower show coming up the same time as that huge accident. Marion goes to those periodically."

"She could pass the baton to Emily," Blake says.

The angels smile. Except one.

As Emily enters the hospital room the next day, she is momentarily mystified by the diffused light filling the space, especially around her mother. Barbara takes a few seconds to realize who she is and speaks with some difficulty.

"Em'ly."

Emily takes her hand. "Mom."

"Angels," Barbara says.

"Angels?"

"I see angels." Barbara looks around at her three angels who are beaming at her. She notices Emily's angels who are beaming, too, but not quite in the same fashion. The humor of the sight gives her a brief surge of energy and clarity. "I see your angels, too. Oh, they're having a wild time with you. Imagine my surprise with that."

"I love you, Mom."

"I love you, too, Emily." Her voice softens and Emily leans over to hear her. "So tired. Ready...for rest...then on...nex' a'venture."

"Go with the angels, Mom. Please say hi to Dad and Lisa for me when you see them, and I know you will."

"My Emily. You...one...most glori'sss treasures...my life."

Emily kisses her mother's hand. "I love you so, so much, Mom."

Her mother's eyes close. She takes a small gasp— was it of delight? probably—and her grasp on Emily's hand loosens. Her crowd of light beings cheers a warm welcome to her as her light body starts to disengage from her physical form.

Emily sets her mother's hand on the bed, but doesn't let go of it. The diffused light has become more luminous; Emily's no longer mystified by it—more like mesmerized by it. She raises her other hand and holds it out in front of her, as if aware of touching gossamer.

Her mother's life force fills the room as she crosses the threshold to the next world. Emily could swear she hears her mother's cries of ecstasy at being reunited with her husband, daughter, parents, and many, many others.

Hours and hours pass; still, Emily remains by her mother's side. The light and palpable energy has faded from the space. Finally, she kisses her mother's hand one last time. After gathering the photographs, vase, and her mother's other personal belongings, she leaves the room. She wonders how the nurses had known to leave her alone, and she notices a special photograph of lilies had been put on her mother's door.

After consulting with the nurses about the next steps regarding her mother's body, Emily climbs into her car and just sits. And sits. And sits. And sits some more. Her angels brace themselves for a wail, but it doesn't come.

Once home, Emily moves the two rocking chairs closer to each other and sits down in one. Her hand reaches out to hold the arm of the other chair. Her angels again brace for a wail, but again it doesn't come.

Emily leans back and shuts her eyes as she basks in the afternoon sunshine. The hand not holding the other chair gravitates to the chest area slightly higher than her heart. Stephanie switches on the sound control for Emily's mind-chatter; she moves the dial to maximum and turns to the rest of the team, eyebrows raised. All is quiet in there.

Wait! There goes a blip of something just as Stephanie starts to turn the dial down. She turns it back up and waits a few seconds. She's about to turn it down again when the blip comes back: "Thank you." The words softly reverberate through Emily's mind over and over.

For the first time, her angels stop performing their tasks and simply meditate.

After giving a final adjustment to the placement of his desk accessories, Jack leans back in the comfy executive chair and gazes out the window. Somewhere out there in the haze, about ten miles away, is the ocean.

This was sure easy, he thinks. (Christopher pats himself on the back.) He's never landed a job this quickly, and he's never had to put ex-con on an application before. He's also never had an ocean view, let alone three—the one here and the two at home. Well, on a clear day that ocean will be in view, he laughs to himself.

His angels had been hard at work on the job front, especially Christopher. With extensive research, they found that a fellow inmate knew someone who knew someone who knew someone, and Jack finds himself now in a high-rise (relatively speaking) office building in Beverly Hills serving several high-end clients. Fun, socially progressive accounts, too—he's never had those before.

But his angels are not resting while he rests at night, of course. They're very hard at work—angelically—arranging events to make sure he's where he's supposed to be on meeting day.

"Have one of his clients meet him across town for lunch."

"Have his boss send him downtown for something."

"Have his ex-wife call him to pick up the kids at that friend's house over there."

"No, he can't have the kids with him that day."

"Oh, no, of course not."

And it continues.

About two miles away, in another cubicle in the great hall, another group of angels is working on a truck driver's life coordinates in conjunction with the life coordinates of those he signed up to have an impact on.

"Okay, when he goes in for the repair, make sure the mechanic misses repairing that other part."

"And who is he going to hit?"

"This car here, which has the schoolteacher in it, which will hit that SUV, which has the fireman in it, which will hit that car over there, which has—"

And sixty miles away, eight feet away, eighty-nine miles away, the angels for other people who will be involved in the accident diligently attend to their charges, too.

In one cubicle: "Well, she wanted to slow down. This will certainly help her do that."

In another cubicle: "He wanted a new car anyway. And his new love-to-be is applying for a job in the dealership down the street from his office."

"Is she supposed to get that job?"

"She is now."

And in another: "She wanted to learn patience. Being in a hospital for a few months will help. And then she can help that handsome, young doctor meet her friend."

And fifty miles away, two hundred miles away, four feet away, in other cubicles, the angels for the people who would be leaving their bodies that day are working diligently, too.

In one cubicle: "Are you sure she's ready to go?"

"No, I'm not sure, but she's sure, and that's what's important here."

"But what about—"

And in another: "But he's always said that he wanted extreme measures taken."

"You know he lied about that, just to appease his wife. But she'll have to draw on power she didn't know she had and become stronger than she ever realized she could."

"But what about—"

And in yet another: "Is that how she'll make the grand exit she's been wanting for so long?"

"She's going to be so happy."

"But she finally got happy here."

"This is always the wildest irony—they can't leave until they're completely okay with staying. Or done whatever other work they came to do. And that can take a lifetime."

"Well, of course it takes a lifetime!"

"True."

"Just some lifetimes are shorter than others."

"True."

"And except when it doesn't."

"Doesn't take a lifetime? True. Some humans come in with that gift or do their work early and can coast the whole time."

"Yeah, all two of 'em!"

And, still, anything can change at any moment because of that flexible flux we call the future. And while death from the human experience isn't exactly *just* yet another step on the pathway, it is just another doorway... as grand as all of the other doorways in all of creation, in all of eternity, in all of infinity.

Four hundred people showed up for Barbara's memorial, about ten percent of the town's population, although there were many from out of town, as well. The formalities were primarily for the other mourners. Emily was barely even mourning. Unlike the other two family deaths and the funerals for so many young or sudden deaths, what a difference it is when someone has reached the end of a full, long, loving life and everything that needed to be said was said. Emily patiently waited to give her respects to her mother after the hubbub of activity and in the most appropriate place: her living room, sitting in one of the rocking chairs, looking out at the garden.

Meanwhile, she ensured the event was a true celebration of her mother's full, long, loving life by requesting that people share their favorite memories of Barbara, the one thing they loved the most about her, not what they wished they had said or anything like that. Actually, as with Emily, everything had all been said.

And Emily senses her mother's happiness. She'd be happy anywhere she found herself in all of creation because that's the choice she made—a choice anyone can make.

"Even you," David says.

"Yes, even me," Emily responds, without knowing her words are a response. Or perhaps she does.

A few days later, she returns to work. As soon as the bell over the door does its ching thing, Marion thrusts a printout of a boarding pass into Emily's hand.

"What's this for?"

"The art-and-flower show in Los Angeles. I can't possibly go this year, and you need to get the Heaven out of here."

"Hey, that should be our line!" David laughs. "At least Marion knows how to follow directions very well."

"Truthfully," Angela says, "she's been giving us directions for a while."

"You leave tomorrow," Marion continues.

"Tomorrow?"

"And stay a while. Relax, have fun, do something different."

On her way home, Emily stops by her lawyer's office to pick up her finalized divorce papers.

That night, as the humans sleep, Brooke fiddles with a few dials on the computer console. The radiant sphere of Earth appears on one of the monitors. "Oh!" she gasps, just as she did when she saw it for the first time. She stares at the spectacular splendor of the globe. From this view, there are no borders, there's no strife—just a magnificent jewel shining brilliantly, suspended in the blackness of the firmament. One tiny piece of heaven in the infinite heavens. One tiny dot of forever in the unified field of forever.

She senses Blake standing behind her. "So what is all this, really? What is life on Earth? Some experiment by some mad scientist?"

"You tell me."

"Well, as Henry once told me, it's a school. But all they have to learn is to *be* all that they are. Just *be* who they really are. They really don't have to *do* much of anything at all. The being will take care of the doing."

David and Angela notice the picture on the monitor and move in closer beside them.

"And are they getting it?" Blake questions Brooke.

"Some have it. More and more are getting it." She stares at the orb of light for a few moments. "It's all given. Everything—love, abundance, harmony—it's all already there. Here. Everywhere. Their only job is to receive it."

"So what's the whole point?" David asks. "I mean really."

"You tell us," Angela says.

"For Infinity to experience every aspect of Itself that It can?"

The senior angels smile.

"If it were up to me," Brooke says, "I certainly wouldn't have designed a world with war, suffering, degradation—none of that."

"How would you have designed it?" Blake asks.

Brooke considers his question. "Well, I guess that wasn't really part of the design, per se. But free will was."

"And aren't those who go to Earth considered the bravest in the whole universe?" David asks.

Six angels speak in unison: "They are."

CHAPTER 7

Whizzing along the freeways heading north and then east from the airport, four unseen passengers in tow, Emily actually appreciates Los Angeles for the first time in her life. A strong wind has cleared the sky, revealing the Hollywood sign and even the Angeles Crest off in the distance. She'd been to the city half a dozen times before, but it was always a rushed, harried trip. And she'd always been, well, Emily—the earlier Emily. The rushed, harried Emily.

And what is this strange feeling that's come over her? Could it be peace? Joy? What in the world is that unusual, foreign sensation?

While Emily decides to give up on trying to figure it out and just enjoy the new...strange...whatever-it-is, David and Angela just enjoy the joyride. Stephanie consults her computer while Jasper whispers. A large, blue pickup truck tailgates Emily's compact rental, which is right behind a large, green van.

"Uh-oh!" Stephanie shouts, instantly bursting the bliss bubble. The other three angels nearly fly out the window in surprise. "Get her out of here—now!"

"Emily, get out of here!" Angela entreats. Jasper adjusts his whispering as well as his volume to the new directive. David attempts, although in vain, to see what has shown up on Stephanie's laptop.

"The karma and intent of the driver behind her has changed," Stephanie explains. "His love meter is so low it's barely registering on the chart at all."

"What the Heaven—?"

"And that really big accident that was supposed to happen?" Stephanie continues. "Not going to. Elements from most of the people have completely changed. Looks like a much smaller one will happen overall, but a really, really bad one is going to happen right ahead here. But it's not meant for her."

"Emily, change lanes," David instructs.

That tailgater has started to annoy her, really messing with her mellow. Emily looks in the left-hand rearview mirror and spots a car barreling down the lane that she would be moving into. She decides to wait for it to pass.

"Emily," David speaks very slowly, very clearly, "this is not the time to be polite. Change lanes right now."

Emily changes lanes, causing the barreling car to swerve into the far left lane. This is Jack! His angels wave wildly to Emily's angels as his car zooms past. Jack glances over, too, but is wearing a far less amicable expression.

Shaking, Jack looks in amazement in his rearview mirror at the crazy, terrible driver who not only cut him off but also almost smashed into him.

At the same time that Stephanie's computer revealed the news, Christopher's computer charts and graphs revealed the change in the whole program around the major accident, too. Rapid-fire, the team bats ideas around Jack's car under Blake's coaching.

"Okay team, think fast!"

"Flat tire!"

"Great idea. How's that play going to happen?"

Christopher stares at his computer screen and then looks up at the road. "A pothole's coming up, straight ahead! Make sure he hits it."

"Distract him," Blake bellows. "Or else he'll swerve to avoid it!"

"Jack," Brooke orders, "look in your mirror and scowl at that crazy, terrible driver again. Now!" Pause. No movement. "I said NOW!"

Jack complies. KERCHUNK! His front left tire hits the enormous pothole. With tremendous care, he steers over to the upcoming exit, miraculously not crashing into any other cars.

Still recovering from her quick lane change and nearly causing an accident, Emily notices a large crate in the middle of the lane she'd just been in. She looks in her rearview mirror just in time to see a very bizarre scenario unfold: The van stops short because of the crate, and the pickup slams into the van at top speed. The car right behind the truck has no chance to stop either, but the cars right behind that one have time to swerve into the other lanes while the cars behind those are able to come to a screeching stop.

Shaking, Emily takes the next exit and pulls over to the side of the road. Jack's rump just happens to be staring her square—or, well, kind of round, really, as the case may be—in the face as he rummages around in his trunk for the jack and spare.

Jack closes the trunk and heads to the front of his car. As he turns to the tire, he notices a very beautiful woman sitting in a car just behind his. Not only is it a little odd to be just sitting in a car on an exit ramp, she's also staring straight ahead, hands locked in a death grip on her steering wheel, and she appears to be hyperventilating. Bewildered, he walks over to her.

"You okay?" he calls through her window.

Emily nods, still trying to catch her breath.

Jack starts to return to his flat tire but turns around to look at her. He walks back to her car. "You sure you're okay?"

Emily nods and, without any consideration of the fact that there's an unknown man standing by her car, she lowers her window. "I'm fine." And then—she wails. Jack's angels put their hands over their ears. Emily's angels put their hands over their faces.

David grimaces. "Way to make a great first impression. Way to go, Emily."

"Maybe it's for the best," Angela sighs. "This way he knows what he's in for, right up front."

"Everything's always for the best," David grouses. "It could just be a little more graceful is all."

"That's our Emily," Stephanie says, "the strong-winded one."

"You never told us about this!" Sapphire grumbles.

"And for very good reason," laughs Brooke. "Can you blame them?"

"Thanks for sharing the wealth!" Christopher groans. "You shouldn't have. No, really—you shouldn't have!"

Once he recovers from his momentary shock over the howling emanating from this woman, Jack leans over and pokes his head in her window. "Can I help you out of your car?"

Emily nods. Jack opens her door. She takes his hand and starts to lift herself out of the car, but then collapses back into her seat. She points to the freeway;

Jack follows the direction her finger is pointing and sees the three-car pileup.

"Oh, wow," Jack exclaims. "I didn't even notice that—all I noticed was my flat tire. I was just there, right there, a minute ago. You, too?"

Emily points out the van and pickup. "I was right between those two!" She wails again. And again.

Jack suppresses the urge to cover his ears. He notices her suitcase in the backseat and figures that her car can be this overly immaculate for only two reasons, and the suitcase doesn't announce that she just left a car detailing service. "A rental car? Are you a long way from home? Tell you what—let me finish changing my tire, then I'll take you for a cold drink. How does that sound?"

"Okay."

"It's probably not too safe for you to just keep sitting in your car, this close to the freeway exit."

"Okay."

Jack watches her emerge—unfold, really, since the car is a compact is Emily is not, height-wise anyway—from her car. He says a long, "Wow!" (silently, to himself, and his angels were very thankful for that small favor) as she slowly straightens up, clutching her car to maintain her balance. "How tall are you?"

Dumbfounded that he would ask such a question at such a time, Emily finishes drawing up to her full height and commences drawing up the wherewithal to answer. "Six feet. Why?"

"Oh, just wondering."

As Jack changes his tire and Emily attempts to steady her stomach, David and Brooke observe a gathering of light beings over the car that had crashed into the back of the truck. Other beings hover over the pickup, as well. The middle-aged woman inside the car slumps over her steering wheel as the whole front end of her car now resembles an accordion.

But her spirit is in ecstasy. "Ohhhhhhhhhh," her spirit self gushes. Her light hands and feet detach from her physical form, followed by her head and then her body. She holds her arms out as if to embrace the cosmos. "So much love!"

Her head angel takes her hands of light. "Of course so much love," he says to her. "That's all there is. That's all you are, Jeannette."

The beings of light start to become visible to her.

"Mom, Dad!" Jeannette cries. "Maggie, Mike! Oh!"

"Are you done here?" the angel asks her.

"Oh, yes," she says. "I'm ready to go home."

"Are you really done?" he demands.

Jeannette hesitates. "Yes. I want to go home. Please take me home!"

"Home is wherever you are," he informs her.

"But it's so beautiful. There's soooooooooooo much love! I can feel it! And there's my family!"

"Your family is everyone around you. Everywhere. It couldn't be any other way."

Jeannette makes no response except to reach out to the love field all around her, so palpable to her in this state. (It's that palpable in every state—if you want to open to it.)

"Have you really finished what you came here for?"

"Yes." But it wasn't very firm.

"All this will always be here, waiting for you. You can always bring this into your life here on Earth. So are you really complete?"

An even longer hesitation. "No."

Sirens blare. Ambulances, fire engines, police cars, and additional emergency trucks race along the shoulder, past the newly formed and growing traffic jam, until they reach the three smashed vehicles.

By the pickup truck, the light beings, which numbered about a hundred, welcome their compadre with rowdy cheers.

Two paramedics approach Jeannette's lifeless form and search for a pulse. "She's gone," says one.

The light beings waiting for Jeannette slowly fade away, but her spirit doesn't want to let go of her angel's hands.

"We're right here," he tells her. "We always have been, we always will be. And all of this will not only be waiting for you at your right time to leave, but it's available now, here, anytime you want it."

He lets go of her hands. Jeannette's hands and feet of light dock and click back into her physical hands and feet; her head slowly follows suit, and then the rest of her light body clicks back into her slumped form.

"No, wait," says the other paramedic. "There's a slight pulse! She's still here."

Jeannette's spirit self notices the EMT tending to her physical self. "Hey," her spirit calls out to her angels. "Maybe he'd be interested in my brother! His partner just dumped him."

"We know," they smile.

"Is this hot one here gay? And single?"

"As a matter of fact, he is. And you thought you were done here!"

"Emily," Emily scolds herself as she drives behind Jack's car, "this Jack could be a descendent of the

Ripper. Yeah, well, at this moment I don't care in the least. He's adorable!" Emily follows his car to a nearby café. Her heart has almost settled back to its normal beat. Almost.

Telling Jack about the events leading up to the pile-up doesn't help it calm down any. They gratefully sip the cold drinks their waiter just set before them.

"No kidding," Jack says. "You were driving along and something told you to change lanes? And then it repeated itself?"

"Yes, and he or she had quite a sense of humor, too. I was going to wait until someone passed me, but whoever was talking said, quite distinctly, 'Emily, this is not the time to be polite, change lanes right now.' So I did. I almost plowed into someone who was coming along behind me, but I sure changed lanes."

"Hang on just a minute! That someone you almost plowed into was me! I had to change lanes to keep from hitting this crazy, terrible—I mean, you, I guess."

They laugh.

"Not so crazy and terrible after all," he smiles.

"Oh, we've only just met," she smiles back. "Give it some time."

"Okay. I'm very happy to do that."

As his smile grows bigger and his eyes shine like the high-beam headlights on a fast-approaching car, Emily suddenly finds the ice cubes in her glass absolutely riveting.

Jack walks Emily to her car in the café's parking lot. "So it's set then? Tomorrow, five o'clock?"

"It's a date," she smiles.

"You know, I could be an ax murderer."

"So could I."

"I could be an ex-con."

"Then we'll certainly have some very interesting conversations."

The next afternoon, after an interminable time at the art-and-flower show and the advertising office and countless glances at clocks, watches, and cell phones, Jack and Emily stroll along the ocean's edge. For hours. Shoes off, they relish the cool waves lapping around their feet.

"Whew, it's hot here," Emily says.

"You look good in hot."

Emily looks at him in delighted surprise. She splashes deeper into the water and then completely immerses herself, clothes be heavened. Jack dives in after her. When he surfaces, he throws his arms around her and kisses her. And kisses her. And kisses her. And she kisses him. And kisses him. And....

"They just met!" Brooke exclaims.

"And your point is?" David asks.

While six angels people watch, angel watch, sky gaze, or look down while attending to their tasks, the two new angels watch the humans closely through all this kissing stuff.

"What do you suppose all the fuss is about?" David asks.

"I'm not sure," Brooke answers. "But look at the rapture on their faces when they come up for air."

"Well, we angels live in rapture all the time."

Brooke watches the humans kiss a little more. "I think their rapture beats ours every day of the week and twice on Sundays."

Emily notices the sun setting over the water—a crimson sun, a cerulean sea.

"I dreamed this once," she sighs to Jack.

Brooke and David watch Jack and Emily gaze into each other's eyes. Brooke gazes into David's eyes, but she sees what she always sees when she looks into anyone's eyes, angel or human—eternity.

Jack and Emily stumble into his apartment, lips still locked on each other's. With unaccustomed aplomb, at least as far as moves on women are concerned, Jack maneuvers her into the living room and onto the couch, where they start to undress each other.

"I've never done this so quickly with anyone before," Emily says, struggling for a breath. "Ever."

"Me either."

"I find that very hard to believe. Look at you. And where you live."

"Believe it."

Jack picks her up and carries her into the bedroom. They fall onto the bed together, arms and legs flailing and entwining. Their laughter is quickly muted by additional kisses on additional places.

Six of their angels turn their backs on them and start to meditate. Brooke and David still want to watch the humans, but they reluctantly turn around after receiving nudges and raised eyebrows from Angela and Blake.

"Jack, Emily, you decent?" Blake and Angela ask together, chortling and slapping their thighs.

Sunned, Brooke and David look at them.

"Sorry," Blake says, trying to wipe the grin from his face.

"Just some angelic humor," Angela guffaws.

"It's a tradition when two angel teams come together in this way for the first time," Blake explains.

"Well, a tradition since humans started worrying about decency, anyway. Of all things to worry about!"

After a couple more snickers from the head angels, the eight angels settle into their meditating.

Brooke opens one eye and catches David trying to look back at the humans. "Hey! We're not supposed to watch."

"Sorry." David's somewhat mortified. "Just really do want to know what all the fuss is about."

But when David has settled into his meditation, Brooke looks over her shoulder at the two humans.

David opens one eye at her, and Brooke catches him catching her sneaking a peek. David returns to his meditation, a big smile on his face. Brooke follows suit. If angels could blush, she would have matched Emily's face right now.

The next morning, Jack awakens with a start. His four angels pop into the room. He caresses Emily's face, and she also awakens with a start. Her four angels pop into the room, as well.

"So you're not a dream after all," Jack whispers to her. "You're not some ethereal being that disappears in the morning light. You're really here."

"In living color," Emily says. "Right here, right now, up close and personal."

"And you are an ethereal being."

"You are, too."

"I dreamed about you. I didn't know who you were or where you lived or what you were doing. I only knew that you were out there somewhere and that I would find you somehow."

Emily smiles at him through her tears. "I know exactly what you mean."

They start to make love again. Their eight angels turn around again.

David leans over to Brooke. "Heard any funny jokes lately?"

"Well, once there were these two angels...."

"I think I've heard that one."

Completely oblivious to their audience of eight, two of whom are especially captivated, Jack drops a strawberry into Emily's mouth.

"Mmmmmmmmmmmmmmmmmm," she says, rolling the strawberry around her mouth.

She drops a strawberry into his mouth.

"Mmmmmmmmmmmmmmmmmmmmmmm."

Jack cuts a bite of his pancake and feeds it to Emily.

"Mmmmmmmmmmmmmmmmmmmmmmmmmmm."

"We're obviously in the monosyllabic stage of the relationship," Angela reports to the others.

"Oh, I don't know about that," Blake chuckles, "I think there were a few syllables in that 'mmmmmmm,' don't you think?"

As the monitor shows Jack and Emily sleeping, their eight angels perform their tasks around their one desk. David surfs the angelnet. He types in "strawberry" and reads the information that appears on the screen.

Angela notices the subject of David's rapt attention and gives him a look. Yes, that kind of look.

"Just wanted to see what all the 'mmmmmmm'ing fuss was about."

Angela raises an eyebrow at Blake, who just smiles. She smiles, too.

Jack and Emily, strolling hand in hand through the mall with their angelic entourage, stop in front of a store window. A very large—*very* large—woman passes the group, and Brooke watches her walk away.

"Speaking of all the fuss around food, what do you suppose makes her eat so much? Why would anyone stuff themselves like that?"

"It's a replacement for unexpressed energy," Blake says. "Those fat cells are really light cells longing to be expressed."

Brooke looks back at the woman. Sure enough, her quadruple chin, arms, legs, belly, and thighs actually do shimmer, but with a strange blue tint.

"I've seen fat angels. Well, not fat fat, like this. But chubby."

"What do you make of that?" Blake asks her.

"Their minds have shaped their bodies," Brooke responds, "just like our human friends here. Every thought becomes part of their shapes. They get what they want."

"Exactly right."

As Brooke wanders over to David, Sapphire sidles over to Blake. "Could you please tell me why they get to, well, you know, when *they* have the questions and *we* have the answers?"

"You know why."

"I'm trying to forget."

"We all get what we sign up for. All of us. Every-where."

Sapphire scowls and returns to her whispering.

"Not very angelic of you," Angela chides her. "And besides, they do have the answers, too, in case you haven't noticed."

"So do the humans, if they'd just shut up long enough to realize it," Sapphire snorts.

Blake and Angela chuckle.

"Actually, it's a really good thing they have no idea how big they are." Sapphire's snort has turned into a hiss. "Can you imagine the mess they'd make across the galaxies with those monkey minds of theirs?"

"Sapphire, you can always change games—I mean assignments," Blake tells her. "You're always at choice. Go ref another game if you want."

Sapphire shrugs.

The human couple wanders into a spiritual-but-not-religious bookstore. Jack spies a picture of Jesus praying, probably in the garden of Gethsemane, while an angel comforts him. He picks it up, moved beyond words.

Emily looks at the picture. "You've felt like that?"

Jack nods.

"Maybe you were held by an angel all those years."

"Maybe. Maybe you were, too."

"Maybe."

Back out in the main mall area, Jack and Emily stroll along a little more and stop in front of another store window. They look at each other with sheer, delighted amazement as they realize what they are looking at:

wedding rings. A bigger smile crosses both of their already smiling faces.

"I had no idea why I was buying all these things," Jack chuckles. "Sesame oil. Capers. Italian herbs. I'd never paid much attention to those things B.P. But the saleswoman in that specialty store on the corner seemed eager to load me up with all these items."

(We're sure you remember that B.P. means Before Prison, right? Thought so.)

"Funny thing. Bet she wanted to show you how to cook, too."

"I was on a mission. Somehow I knew you were going to burst into my life."

Emily lights the candles on the table, beautifully set with Jack's long-unused family heirloom china and silverware. A vase of red roses sits between the crystal candleholders. The sun setting over the ocean fills the room with a red hue as the pair starts to serve the semi-gourmet feast they've prepared for themselves.

In the background, Barry White accompanies them. Jack grabs the bottle of Chardonnay and sings into the top of it, as if into a microphone. "You'll never find...as long as you live...Someone who loves you tender like I-I-I-I-I-I do!"

"But aren't they breaking up in that song?"

"Uhhhhhhh, not in our version of it."

He swirls and swoops her around the kitchen, ending in a low dip. "And you just found...the life of your love!"

"The love of my life, you mean?" Emily laughs. "Actually, I like your way much better. Kind of flows with the go."

"Goes with the—nah, I like your way much better."

After the first course of walnut-and-goat-cheese salad with raspberry vinaigrette comes lemon-caper grilled salmon with herb risotto and grilled asparagus under a dollop of hollandaise sauce. The feast is followed by, yes, strawberries...dipped in chocolate.

"Ohhhhhhhh, again with the strawberries!" whines Brooke as the humans drop the strawberries into the other's mouth at a speed that would test the patience of a sloth.

"Chocolate is the best invention ever in the history of ever," Emily swoons.

"Almost the best invention."

"The best food invention," she smiles.

"Really?" Brooke asks.

"Really," Emily adds.

As Gladys Knight croons softly in the background, Jack and Emily slow dance. "You're the best thing that ever happened to me," Jack softly sings in Emily's ear. He spins her into another deep dip, followed by a long, passionate kiss. He whisks her off to the bedroom.

"Hey—" Angela starts.

"Enough with the jokes," grumbles David. Five angels smile, but two others want to grumble, too.

After a perfunctory handshake at her introduction to Emily, Lacey quickly leaves to return to her empty house. Dick has left her already, but you probably saw that one coming.

Emily squats down to greet Ben and Chelsea. Each offers her a hand, which she takes in her hands. The four walk into the apartment, accompanied by their fourteen angels (four for each adult, three for each child, all at their tasks). Brooke and David watch Jack and Emily very carefully, enthralled by these humans in love—in love with this amazing other, with these amazing children, with this amazing life, with the amazing grace of it all.

That night, the three introduce their fourth to the fun of pre-bedtime. After the children fall asleep, the couple settles in the living room. Emily leans her head on Jack's shoulder. "You know something? I dreamed about them almost as much as I dreamed about you." She looks up, gazing adoringly at him.

Jack's heart swells with love for her as well as with relief that this first time together had passed so beautifully for all four of them. He notices Emily continuing to gaze at him, but he can tell that she's not really seeing him. "What?"

But Emily can't quite put it into words yet. At the moment Jack noticed her strange stare, she had been seeing....well, a vista. Before her eyes, as she was looking at Jack's face, she saw the rest of her life stretching out before her—a life filled with the love of a mate and children, filled with walks along the beach instead of hikes in the mountains, filled with a quiet mind, filled with a heart overflowing with gratitude.

Without a word, Jack sees the vista, too.

Jack and Emily drive through the L.A. smog toward the Staples Center. Brooke and David look with horror at the filthy atmosphere.

"It'll all get done," Angela assures the two relative neophytes. "They have eternity."

"Doesn't mean they don't do what they can do now," David says. "If a human is aware, he or she has a huge responsibility."

"Much more than if they were just asleep and didn't know any better," Brooke adds.

"I don't mean fretting about it," David says.

"No, angst only makes things worse, of course," Brooke agrees. "But tackling it with calm certainty and love would get it done."

"Especially love," David says.

Yet again, Blake and Angela raise their eyebrows; yet again, they're impressed.

As the couple enters the sports arena, Brooke and David shake their heads in disbelief. Every person has at least three, sometimes four angels, so there are over eighty thousand beings in the center.

When Jack, Emily, and the crowd around them jump to their feet, cheering on the Lakers, Brooke and David jump to their feet, too.

"You're angels!" Angela scolds them. "You cheer for both sides! Unless a specific win is necessary for your assignment, of course."

"Oh, right," the novices both say, somewhat dismayed...although probably more dismayed that they can't participate than that they were caught in human-like behavior.

"Just watch your humans!"

Brooke and David turn their attention back to Jack and Emily....And then sneak a peek at the game as the crowd roars again.

Chopsticks in hand, Jack and Emily munch on take-out Chinese food straight from the cartons. While luxuriating in the bathtub.

"And you have no animosity?" Emily asks him.

"No," Jack says. "But I certainly feel like I've paid my dues for life. First a very unhappy marriage. Then that."

"But three years of your life! And your children were without their father for three years."

"They have me now, much better than before. And now I feel like I got first pick in the NBA draft."

Emily smiles through her blushing. "And I suppose you and Dick arranged all of that back when you were having tea in the ethers."

"And I suppose you and I arranged all of this back when we were having tea in the ethers."

"No, I don't suppose it. I know we did."

The angels have their backs turned to the pair.

David turns to Brooke. "Haven't I seen you here before?"

The expression she gives him is so wry it can't even be called a smile.

"I've been waiting for you my whole life," Jack whispers to Emily early the next morning.

"Same here," she whispers back. "By the way...just for the record...in case you were wondering—"

"Yes, what are you stalling about?"

"Well, are you going to ask me to marry you? Because if you are, I'd say yes."

She dives under the covers to hide her face. After recovering from his momentary shock, Jack dives after her.

In a very fine restaurant, some very fine wine is poured by a very fine waiter for a very fine couple. They clink their glasses, although the toast is made only with their eyes.

Jack points out the window. "What's that?"

Emily tries to figure out what he was pointing at, and when she turns back to ask him, a distinctive small jewelry box sits on the table before her.

She jumps up and grabs him. "Yes! Yes! Yes!"

"I haven't even asked you yet!"

"Yes! Yes! Yes!"

"Emily, can you sit your delectable derriere back down?" She sits down again, but probably still with some air between the chair and her delectable derriere. "Emily, will you marry me?"

"Oh, yesssssss!" she cries.

Jack slides the ring on her finger, and they kiss amidst many smiles from the diners around them.

The next day, they head back to the mall to buy those wedding rings they'd found themselves looking at just a week prior, which had been just two days after they met. After they purchase the rings, they pack up a Jeep borrowed from a friend of Jack's—Emily's rental had long since been returned—for a trip to Idaho...with a stop in Las Vegas on the way.

A little fast? No chance. Well, it might've been for some, but not in this case. Remember those forty qualities that Jack listed with such deliberation? Emily is or has all forty of them. The last thing on his list was, "She has her own list of all the qualities she wants in her mate, and I surpass them all."

She didn't have many items on her list: "Spiritual powerhouse. Family man. Gets me." Well, perhaps that last one entails forty items in itself.

But they'd also done their work, put in their time in so many ways, and neither of them *needed* it to happen. That's usually when it does.

CHAPTER 8

The sleep-and-dream monitor displays Jack and Emily sound asleep, wrapped in each other's arms in their Las Vegas hotel room. The night has already brought a visit from the angels to the hotel, where they could *not* watch their humans, followed by a return to the great hall. As the humans seem to have finally calmed down from their wedding night, the eight angels huddle around the desk performing their assorted tasks. Kind of.

Sapphire looks over the top of Christopher's laptop at Brooke, a slight scowl marring her features. Then she sighs, relaxing her face.

Brooke glances over at her, but she has returned to her whispering. Brooke turns to Christopher, who smiles at her.

"Christopher," Brooke asks, "what do you make of all the bad things that happen on Earth?"

"Oh, humans tend to be generally good. Some just get sidetracked along their way to 'good,' I guess." Christopher lets her think about that for a moment before asking, "Feel like playing some games?"

"Sure."

David joins them as Christopher pulls up a picture of the globe. From a pull-down menu, he selects a filter.

They watch a greyish-black web extend all around the planet.

"That's the dark side. It gets lighter every year."

"Dark side?" David coughs. And just like Brooke said a long time ago, he says, "There's no such thing."

"Right, it's not a real thing, per se. It's just people's belief in it that creates it. There are no monsters, no creepy crawlies, really, not anywhere—not out in the universe and not inside any human heart."

Christopher selects another filter from the pull-down menu, and the group watches Earth light up under a rose-colored web.

"That's the angelic realm," he explains. "It stays exactly the same, wherever we are—whatever planet in whatever galaxy—millennium after millennium, light-year after light-year. We're already infinite love, so it stays steady. It won't grow or shrink or become lighter or darker."

Christopher picks another filter, and they watch a glorious golden grid form over the planet. "That's the awakening," he says. "More and more humans are awakening. Every single day, the grid—and the planet—gets lighter and lighter, plus more and more powerful, too. It's better here than anywhere else in the universe. Some planets are more awake, but they started out more awake. These humans on Earth are singular in this capacity."

As Christopher talks, the golden web glows a little brighter, then even a little brighter again.

"There's only so much we angels can do," Christopher adds. "We are created only to love and only to be love. But humans start out their first time with almost nothing, and they have an infinite capacity to grow, time after time, so the more their love grows—"

"The brighter the web grows," Brooke finishes.

"The higher they vibrate, the more people they get to vibrate at that level. Once one breaks through to a new level, others further on down the road can get there in even less time."

"How much brighter has it become just while we've been standing here watching it?" David queries.

"About three percent," Christopher says, pointing to a gauge in the corner of the screen. "You should've seen it five thousand years ago, two thousand years ago. Even a hundred years ago. So much darker."

"How much brighter will it get?" Brooke asks.

"Up to them," Christopher responds, pointing to the planet under the grid. He watches Brooke and David, to determine their reactions to his words. They are transfixed by the picture on the screen.

Christopher switches back and forth between the different light grids. "You can see the webs without the computer," he adds, "if you want to. Anyone can, even them."

Brooke and David remain completely transfixed, spellbound by the images on the computer.

Christopher smiles. The other angels stop their work—watching, loving, whispering, loving, computing, loving, assessing, loving, determining, and loving some more—and smile at them, as well.

"Uh oh, they're waking up again."

Another visit. Another round of jokes while they have their backs turned to their human charges on their wedding night. And another return to the great hall.

While the sleep-and-dream monitor reveals Jack and Emily sleeping and dreaming—once again—in their hotel room, Brooke watches a quick recap of the world news on a special section of the angelnet. She then turns to a talk show taken from human cable television.

"What are you doing?" Blake asks her.

"Oh, just always want to see if I can understand them better."

"Well, that's good."

Brooke watches the show for a few minutes. "Can you believe humans ever complain, even for a second? Not the ones who are having an especially hard time of it, but the ones who are having an especially good time of it. Actually, the ones who have a harder time of it seem to complain less. But if I were there, I would never complain. Ever."

She stops as she notices the other angels staring at her. "Well, can you imagine what it would be like to feel rain on your skin, fall asleep in your beloved's arms, make love, eat a strawberry, taste chocolate? Just being able to experience that would be worth the price of admission, to me."

She looks again at the teams of angels who are still just looking at her, mildly amused.

"What?"

They continue smiling at her.

"No one understands."

"I do," David says.

She looks at him, and then quickly looks away, back to the monitor.

The other angels keep smiling to themselves. Even Sapphire seems to be out of her funk of late. Blake and Angela look at each other—and nod.

"Okay Brooke and David," Blake announces, "it's Big Game time. Time for an introduction. Ready to meet the Big Boss?"

After a few seconds of stunned silence, the two gasp. "Finally!"

"I'd love to. But, just out of curiosity, why now of all times?" Brooke asks. "The humans are doing so well. We don't really need to ask anything. For once, we don't really need any help to figure out a course of action."

"You'll see."

Angela adjusts a special dial under Emily's monitors. David watches over her shoulder as he prepares himself—straightens his collar, brushes some angel dust off of his shirt—to be at his best for this long-awaited introduction.

Meanwhile, Blake adjusts a special dial under Jack's monitors. Brooke watches over his shoulder as she prepares herself—stands up a little straighter, fluffs up her aura—to be at her best for this most auspicious moment.

And who appears on that special monitor, looking right at David is...Emily!

And who appears on that special monitor, looking right at Brooke, is...Jack!

"U-u-u-u-ummmmm...." David stammers.

"U-u-u-u-ummmmm...." Brooke stammers.

"You were expecting someone else?" laugh Blake and Angela.

"U-u-u-u-uh, well, yeah."

"U-u-u-u-uh huh."

Emily and Jack smile at the not-so-new-anymore angels from their monitors. Brooke and David look to the upper-left monitor to find the two humans are still sound asleep, still wrapped in each other's arms.

"U-u-u-u-uh..." the two angels say in unison.

"Hi, Brooke and David," Emily says.

"We want to thank you so very, very, very much for everything you've done for us," Jack says.

"Everything!" Emily adds.

"U-u-u-u-u-u-u-u-u-uh...." The two angels certainly don't have much else to say for the time being.

Jack and Emily give them both a warm smile from the monitors. The angels look back at the sleeping versions of these humans. And back to the humans looking at them from the other side of the monitors. And back to the sleeping forms. And back....

"Who did you think we were talking to when we said we were talking to the Big Boss?" Blake asks.

"Uuuuuuuuh, well, G-G-God, or s-s-s-someone like that." David doesn't usually stutter, but this moment seems to be calling for it.

"The Big Kahuna?" Brooke doesn't usually giggle, but this moment seems to be calling for it.

"Well, we were. Always."

"Then...who...is...." David isn't usually at a loss for words.

"God, really?" Brooke finishes for him.

"Everything," Angela answers. "Everything everywhere. The whole of everything and the loving principle that guides all of creation."

"But in this ball game," and of course you know that's Blake using those terms, "the humans are the ones who are really in charge of the playing field, the playbook, the scorecard, each play. Each time, every time, every minute of their lives."

"Thanks again, Brooke and David," Emily says.

"For everything," Jack says.

Brooke and David are still not quite aware that they can talk to these two humans directly in this particular moment of infinity.

"Then w-w-w-what in c-c-c-c-creation do they need angels f-f-for?" Brooke sputters.

"It's a team sport," Blake says. "No one does this alone. When they go to Earth, they need help remembering. Everyone needs a coach. It's all part of the game."

"What a game!" David says.

"But most players of a game know what the game entails, what the rules are," Brooke says.

"They do," Angela states. "Before they sign up, they definitely know the rules of the game."

"We didn't." It was almost a whine, but David is too perplexed to let loose a really good one.

"True," Blake says.

"Everything's for a reason," Angela adds.

"To go play the Earth game requires some serious, serious in-depth training."

"Seriously."

The other six angels leave Brooke and David alone for the rest of the night. After the monitors of the higher Jack and Emily are shut off, Brooke and David watch—just stare at, really—the sleeping Jack and Emily. For the most part, that is. A couple of times, they switch on the day-in-review monitors to watch their wedding again.

Emily and Jack stand before an elderly justice of the peace in a tiny, flower-filled chapel as an elderly woman plays an organ behind them. After the radiating-from-the-inside-out bride and groom exchange wedding rings, they kiss.

All eight disappear when the humans start to stir...

...and reappear in their assignments' hotel room.

Jack and Emily wrap their arms around each other...and then kiss...and then start to make love. The angels politely turn around.

Angela snorts. "You hear one about the humans on the morning after their wedding—"

"We're living that one," David moans.

"Indeed," Angela says.

"But they were only living at half wattage. Not even that high," David says.

"And they knew that." Brooke is flummoxed, as well. "At least their higher selves did."

"Their human selves seem to be making up for it now," David says.

"One of the best games in the entire universe," Blake chuckles.

"Most humans live at less than half of their half of their half of their half," Stephanie comments.

"That's a lot of halves," notes David.

"Most live at less than five percent capacity," Stephanie says.

Behind them, Emily moans with pleasure. For quite a while.

"Must be nice," Brooke says.

At noon, the newlyweds fall asleep again. The angels disappear...

...and return to their desks in the great hall, completely unaccustomed to being there at this time of day. An entirely different shift of angels surrounds them. But, as the angels see on the monitor, Emily rolls over and bumps into Jack.

"Uh oh," Blake says. "Here we go again."

The angels disappear...

...and reappear in their humans' hotel room, where the drawn shades have the room as dark as night, but the pillowtalk stopping and the kissing starting alert the group that it's time to turn around again.

"Good thing we don't require overtime pay," Brooke says.

"Good thing we don't need sleep," David adds.

"Good thing we're angels and completely devoted to our jobs," Angela chides.

Somewhat ashamed, Brooke and David just nod; the other angels smile.

In the rugged mountains of Idaho—none too soon for Brooke and David, who had grown weary of the revolving door from the hotel room to the great hall—Emily and Jack take the highway exit near Emily's house. They stop at the nearby convenience store to gas up and purchase snacks. As they are climbing back into the Jeep, the very same robber that David saw on his first day on Earth enters the store and pulls his gun on the owner again. Both men are older now, of course, and the meth usage has decimated the robber's teeth.

"Give me your money," he barks.

The store owner speaks with resolve through his shaking. "No. I'm giving you a phone number."

The robber almost drops his gun. "Are you kidding me? I could kill you!"

"I'm going to save your life." The owner holds out a slip of paper with a phone number on it. "Call him. He got off meth over ten years ago now. It sure ain't easy, but you can do it, too. I know you can."

The robber does indeed drop his gun. After a moment, however, he grabs the slip of paper.

All six of their angels cheer as they high five and fist bump each other.

As the robber leaves, his angels follow, blowing kisses and waving to the store owner's angels.

Jack and Emily pull out of the parking lot. Their angels wave to the other angel teams and give them a thumbs-up—times eight.

Just as Beth, Emily's longtime friend and a real estate agent, finishes pounding the "For Sale" sign into the ground, Emily and Jack pull up to the house. Emily fights back tears as she waves to her friend and looks up at her former home.

Jack takes her hand. "We'll be back, if you want. Ten years will fly by. You know, Lacey...."

"I know. Hey, maybe Chelsea is truly gifted and will graduate early." Emily tries to laugh and tightens her grip on his hand. "We'll be happy wherever we are," she says to him.

In the midst of packing, Emily stands and, putting her hands on her hips, bends from side to side to stretch out her back. Sam had taken only his personal items, and Beth told her friend that she could sell the furniture for her once the house was sold, so there isn't all that much to pack. All of the yard and garden tools, the snowblower, and many other things that they won't need in L.A. can be left for the new homeowners. But heirlooms and her special kitchenware? Definitely going with her.

"Take a break?" Jack asks.

"Sure."

Without even saying a word, they move the rocking chairs right next to each other and take a seat, soaking in the afternoon sunshine.

Jack takes her hand. "You could make a beautiful home in a hut, on Mars, in a tent, anywhere. You certainly have the knack. And we'll come back here if you want."

Emily smiles at him, appreciating his gesture. "We'll see."

"Darling homes can be created wherever you go," Jack says. "Because you happen to be the darling in the equation. You put the darling in *darling*."

"Have I told you lately that I love you?"

"Yes. Every minute we've been together."

"Same goes for you."

Jack kisses her hand. "So, like I said, we can come back here."

"Well, we'll see," Emily repeats. "I'm open to all good possibilities. And they're all good as long as they're with you."

Emily and Jack load the last of her boxes into a trailer. She takes a final look at her sweet house with its lavish gardens, and she puts her hand over her heart. Jack touches her elbow, and she throws her arms around him, choking back a sob. He holds her in a long hug until she feels ready to leave.

Jack pulls the Jeep and trailer up in front of the flower shop at Emily's direction. Marion stands in the doorway, her smile and radiance broadcasting the warm welcome they always have.

"Marion, this is the only man worth leaving all of this for."

Marion smiles at him. "I knew you'd have to be special, and of course you are."

She hands Emily an envelope.

"What's this?" Emily asks.

"Open it and find out."

Inside is a check for five thousand dollars from... Veronica. On the card, Veronica has written two words: "Thank you." Behind the card is a check in the same amount from Marion.

"She gave the same to me, and I'm giving it to you. An auspicious start to your new life in Los Angeles," Marion grins.

Emily fights back tears. "I wish I could stay—and go."

"Learn to bilocate. At least until the children are in college."

They laugh.

"Then we might come back here," Jack says. "This is paradise."

Emily gives one more hug to Marion as well as to her cats, who had been staying at the flower shop in her absence. Now they would be staying there for the rest of their lives—and loving Marion and her environs far more than they would a big-city apartment.

Jack pulls away from the curb as Emily waves good-bye to Marion. The two women continue waving until the Jeep rounds a corner and they can no longer see each other.

Emily returns from the women's room at a rest stop, wiping away a tear. As she spies Jack leaning against the Jeep, watching her, a huge smile spreads across her face.

She takes the keys he holds out and settles into the driver's seat. In the passenger's seat, Jack playfully puts his chin in his hands, elbows on the center console, and stares at her.

"Silly guy."

"That'd be me."

"Do you believe in angels?"

"Of course I do. I have to. I'm looking at one right here, right now."

She smiles and looks over at him. "Funny, so am I." She thinks for a moment. "Marion is an angel."

"Takes one to know one."

Just for the record, you're wrapped in the arms of love when you're born, you're wrapped in the arms of love when you die, you're wrapped in the arms of love now, you're wrapped in the arms of love always. You don't need to look for love. Love is what you look with. It's all that you are. Love of another human is just the recognition of this love.

Just sayin'.

CHAPTER 9

As Jack and Emily sleep, snuggled together in a motel room still on the way back to L.A., Brooke and David surf the angelnet together.

"Oh, these wild humans," David groans. "Every time they take one step forward, they take another step back. The Berlin Wall came down. Great. The Soviet Union disassembled. Great. But the stockpile of guns were sold to countries in Africa, where they were used in massive civil unrest. That's just one example. There are hundreds more. Thousands."

"It's crazy. I wish I could go and make it different. I'd listen to my angels."

"Yeah, me, too."

"Sure you would," say Blake and Angela.

As Jack drives through the mountains just outside of L.A. and their eight angels attend to their tasks, Emily studies the stars. "Do you believe everything is getting better?" she asks Jack.

"Of course. Look at what just happened to us."

"I mean for the world in general."

"Yes. But sometimes it's hard to keep thinking that way."

"Sure is."

"Sometimes it's enough to make someone want to go crazy."

"Sometimes I look at it all from a higher perspective. Kind of like, 'Oh, how interesting. How absolutely fascinating. What a strange thing they're doing—killing each other in the name of God. Stopping the food from reaching the hungry. What a strange thing to be doing!' I don't mean it in a coldhearted way, more as a fascination in the machinations of the heart of these confused beings also known as humans. Kind of like parents looking at their children, knowing that they'll know better someday."

Jack nods.

Emily and David both speak at the same time: "It's a young planet."

Jack and Brooke both speak at the same time: "It is."

Brooke and David look at each other, then at their teammates, then at each other again.

"Did they just say—"

"I think they did."

A look of great appreciation passes over Brooke's face and then David's, too—they're very impressed with these two human things. Meanwhile, the other angels are very impressed with these two angelic things.

"And then," Emily continues, "I try to put myself in the place of the mother trying to feed her children. I also try to put myself in the place of the warlord trying to keep the food for himself. There must be a reason he's doing it. Greed, which is from fear, of course, but there must be something else. Keeping things from others means that he's keeping something from himself, too, in a way. And if everything's moving to a higher good, this must be part of it. Somehow."

"Perhaps it's all an act," Jack suggests. "Former presidents, dictators, despots—everything is a shadow play that the whole world chooses to participate in. We all have it by the right of our mind-sets. Some of the actors work to change the ending of the play, but not many."

"More and more. Did you know that tiny, poor, war-torn countries sometimes send money for relief aid to the U.S. after it experiences a natural disaster? After 9/11, too."

Jack takes her hand and kisses it. "It's way beyond wonderful to be able to talk like this. And to love the one I'm talking to.

"It sure is," Emily agrees. "Oh, it sure is."

Back at the L.A. apartment, Emily starts to put the rocking chairs by the living room window. Jack taps her on the shoulder and motions for her to follow him to Ben's room. Since the shades are drawn, at first she can't see anything in the semi-gloom, but then—there it is. A loveseat. Of course! Emily laughs. She'd told him about the rocking chairs long before their trip, and they were fine for her mother and her, but oh how things change.

They carry the love seat from its hiding place into the living room and place it in front of the window. They fall into the deep cushions and just hold each other. After a few minutes of listening to the other's breathing, the other's heartbeat, Jack lifts her face to his. They gaze at each other with unabashed love, adoration, wonder, reverence, joy, and, well, the list could go on and on. They finally found each other. It does happen.

Brooke and David watch Jack and Emily's faces closely, with wonder and, perhaps, some envy. Angelic envy.

Meanwhile, on the other side of town, a delivery man hands a bouquet of flowers to a very surprised Dick. He's even more surprised and confused when he reads the card: "Thank you for all you've done."

It's signed, "A Grateful Acquaintance."

The monitor shows Jack and Emily sleeping. David drums his fingers as Brooke paces. The other angels attend to their tasks, but furtively sneak glances at the two jumpy ones.

"Not very angelic of you," David says to Brooke, referring to her pacing.

She stops pacing and points to his drumming fingers. "Nor you."

He stops drumming.

"You know," he says, "we love all the time. But we have nothing to compare it to."

"Humans have no idea what they have."

Blake points to Jack and Emily. "Some do."

"It's the only place in the universe where you can put your love into physical expression," David extols. "I want to taste the tang of a strawberry. I want to touch someone. In other places, the beings either have no interest in that or they merge as one with the strawberry or the other being. Physicality is where it's at."

"Sure is."

"So what are you waiting for?" Blake asks.

Brooke turns around and looks at him. "Huh?"

"What are you waiting for?" Angela asks.

"Huh?" That was David's turn.

Brooke and David look around at the other angels, who have stopped their computing and whispering and are just looking at them.

Stephanie, Christopher, Sapphire, and Jasper speak in unison. "What are you waiting for?"

"You think you came here to teach them?" Angela whoops. "They're actually here to teach you. And now you're ready to go. So go."

Brooke and David also speak in unison. "Say what?"

"Why do you think advanced humans get a fourth angel?" Blake queries them. "It's not for the humans—they've already got it!"

Brooke and David still....don't....quite....get...it.

Sapphire whispers to them. "The assignment is for you, not them."

Jasper takes a different approach and holds his hands to his mouth, megaphone style. "Earth to angels! Earth to angels!" He puts his hands down. "You think you were here for them. But they were here for you."

"They'll get it," Blake smiles. "They have eternity."

Brooke and David gasp in surprise. They look at each other in sheer ecstasy...clasp hands together...and disappear.

David stands before Penelope's desk.

Penelope crosses her arms and wrinkles her face. "What in the world would you want to go back there for—as a human? You, more than most, can see how hard it is."

"Oh, no, you don't! The jig is up. I know what's been going on."

Penelope smiles. "I still had to ask. Just to make sure."

Brooke stands before Henry's desk.

"But we get to live in rapture all the time," Henry protests. "They only get it on occasion."

"Which makes it all the more special. And don't you try to stop me. I know what's going on."

Henry smiles. "We don't send just anybody there, you know."

"I know that now!"

David still stands before Penelope's desk.

"Of course you can go," Penelope says. "What do you think you've been being trained for? It takes a very special being to handle life on Earth."

David smiles. "I know. A verrrrrry special being."

Brooke still stands before Henry's desk.

"Of course you can go," Henry says. "What do you think you've been being trained for? It takes a very special being to handle life on Earth."

Brooke smiles. "I know. A verrrrrry special being."

David still stands before Penelope's desk listening to her lecture. "And when you start out, you're going to be one of those people who—"

Brooke still stands before Henry's desk listening to his lecture.
"—doesn't have a clue."

David still stands before Penelope's desk as she says, "You'll start out—"

Brooke still stands before Henry's desk as he shakes his head, "—way, way worse than Jack."

"—way, way worse than Emily," Penelope says to David.

"But you have to get—" Henry says to Brooke.

Penelope shrugs, "—your feet wet."

Henry shrugs, "—your wings in shape to fly."

"You'll forget everything we taught you," Penelope sighs.

"And your job will be to remember," Henry says, pointing at Brooke.

"—remember what's so obvious, up here, and what you already know, way deep inside, down there," Penelope laughs.

Henry crosses his arms. "To love—"

"—and then love some more," Penelope says.

"And, at some point—"

"—remember," says Penelope.

"And then love some more again," says Henry.

"And wake up," Penelope says.

"And you will—that's the whole point. Someday, anyway." Henry smiles at Brooke.

"But it's going to take quite a few lifetimes to get ready for her," Penelope warns.

"You have to put in your time before you can meet up with him," Henry cautions. "It could take many, many lifetimes."

"Whatever it takes!" David says. "Time to laugh and let laugh."

"That's live and let live," Penelope corrects him, but then ponders for a moment. "Well, as always, the way you have it is probably more accurate."

"I'll wait," Brooke says. "However long."

Henry nods his head. Brooke throws her arms around this big, old, sloppy angelic bear in a big, old, sloppy angelic bear hug.

"Time to go learn and live."

"Live and lear—nah, your way is better."

"The whole point is that I can't get it wrong."

"And, of course, once you know that, David, you have the opportunity and responsibility to get it right. Really right."

"I know you won't be far. And there's only love. So there's nowhere else I can possibly go."

"Right, Brooke. But it might take a long, long time to remember that."

So, okay, let's just skip all those lifetimes where they didn't quite get it, shall we? You know what they're like. You've lived a few thousand of them yourself, but if you're reading this story, your life is no longer in that category. Your life is less clunky, more streamlined, more gracious. Yes, that's you.

The year is 2458. A baby boy is born. You might think the hospital delivery room is very high tech, but it's not—not at all. It looks like a room your great-, great-, great-, great- grandmother would have had your great-, great-, great-grandmother in: warm, dark, quiet, a few women gently guiding the mother through the delivery. Sometimes low tech is the highest tech there is. The only major difference between this room in the future and the room of the 1800s is that the father is present, as well, of course.

And now the year is 2461. A baby girl is born in a not-so-very-high-tech delivery room. You would recognize one of the midwives—Sapphire.

Fast-forward through all the learning to crawl, all the bumping into walls, all the Christmas presents under the tree (some traditions are worth staying the same in the future), getting hit in the back of the head with the ultrateeter teeter-totter. (We didn't say life would be totally perfect, did we? Not even close. What'd be the point in that? That's how David decided to be a pediatrician; his getting stitches was an abysmal experience. That's often what abysmal experiences are for: to transform things.) In the street—well, about those streets....Cars have been replaced with little hydrogen flying machines, and every home has a landing pad instead of a driveway. The school blackboards are now giant computer screens that can be written on with a finger and erased with the palm of a hand. A boy presents a report to his class. Fast-forward to an eighteen-year-old girl giving the valedictorian's speech at her high-school commencement. Fast-forward to a twenty-two-year-old man graduating from college and being handed the keys to his own flying machine.

And slowing down for just a minute, a cozy church, filled to overflowing with flowers, is also filled to overflowing with guests. After making sure that the corsages are perfect on the groomsmen, then that the bouquet is perfect, Brooke, a wedding floral designer with far more renown and respect than her twenty-five years on Earth would warrant, takes her seat. The music starts, and the guests turn to watch the flower girl dropping red rose petals down the aisle. As the little girl passes her, Brooke notices a very handsome man across the aisle. He seems to be just a few years older, but it's kind of hard to look at him because he's smiling at her with eyes shining like the high beams on her hydrogen plane—a lot to look at.

A few hours later, after hors d'oeuvres, dinner, drinks, cake-cutting, and one, two, three, fourteen dances—for Brooke and David, that is, not the newlyweds—we see an ecstatic bride and groom waving goodbye to their guests. They leave the wedding reception in an overly decorated hydrogen plane—complete with cans and streamers and "Just Married" in the back window. The cans clunk in the breeze, if not along the roadway anymore.

Amidst the throng of well-wishers, David turns to Brooke. She smiles. He smiles back.

And a little later, we see her fumbling as she presses her hand to the scanner to open her door (no more keys) at her apartment. After the fumbling settles down and the door finally gets opened, she leads him into her living room. A love seat sits in a large bay window. David takes her in his arms and, after crashing to the love seat, kisses her. And kisses her. And kisses her. And....

Well, you get the idea. It's happily ever. It does happen. Really.

ACKNOWLEDGEMENTS

We all have so many teachers and angels along this amazing journey—way too many to list anywhere except in the heart. I want to say thank you to *all* of my teachers, especially Rev. Dr. Michael Bernard Beckwith, Rev. Karyl Huntley, the late Doris Jones, Lavandar, and Jim Self.

A very, very special thank you goes to my very, very special BFF/sistergirlfriendangels: Barbara Cox, Betsey Crawford, Rev. Lee McNeil Nash, Grace Sears, Dana Swift, and Jenni Lipari Tatarsky. You are the angels of my life.

Thank you to my champions: Eileen Duhné, Deborah Erwin, David Goldberg, Barry Goldstein, Ariel Grey, Patrice Karst, Jaclyn Anjee Lang, Christopher and Jessica Loving-Campos, Angela Melia, Jennifer Peeso, Pete Shaffner, Barbara St. John, Mark Waldman, Kiara Windrider, and the rest of my angelic coworkers at Centers for Spiritual Living Home Office. Eugene Holden, thank you for your wonderful way of making "every day a holiday and every meal a banquet."

Marion, this book is dedicated to *you*. Thank you for sharing your wisdom, love, and light so generously and for bringing Heaven to Earth.

Most of all, thank you to my beloved husband Steve. It's not just "our song"—you truly are the best, best, best thing that ever, ever, ever happened to me.

In loving memory of

David Krull